READ ALL THE MYSTERIES IN THE
HARDY BOYS ADVENTURES:

#1 *Secret of the Red Arrow*

#2 *Mystery of the Phantom Heist*

#3 *The Vanishing Game*

#4 *Into Thin Air*

#5 *Peril at Granite Peak*

#6 *The Battle of Bayport*

#7 *Shadows at Predator Reef*

COMING SOON:

#9 *The Curse of the Ancient Emerald*

DECEPTION ON THE SET

#8 *DECEPTION ON THE SET*

FRANKLIN W. DIXON

ALADDIN New York London Toronto Sydney New Delhi

ALADDIN

An imprint of Simon & Schuster Children's Publishing Division
1230 Avenue of the Americas, New York, NY 10020
This Aladdin hardcover edition February 2015
Text copyright © 2015 by Simon & Schuster, Inc.
Jacket illustration copyright © 2015 by Kevin Keele
All rights reserved, including the right of reproduction in whole or in part in any form.
ALADDIN is a trademark of Simon & Schuster, Inc.,
and related logo is a registered trademark of Simon & Schuster, Inc.
THE HARDY BOYS MYSTERY STORIES, HARDY BOYS ADVENTURES,
and related logo are trademarks of Simon & Schuster, Inc.
Also available in an Aladdin paperback edition.
For information about special discounts for bulk purchases, please contact
Simon & Schuster Special Sales at 1-866-506-1949 or business@simonandschuster.com.
The Simon & Schuster Speakers Bureau can bring authors to your live event.
For more information or to book an event contact the Simon & Schuster Speakers Bureau
at 1-866-248-3049 or visit our website at www.simonspeakers.com.
Jacket design by Karin Paprocki
The text of this book was set in Adobe Caslon Pro.
Manufactured in the United States of America 0115 FFG
2 4 6 8 10 9 7 5 3 1
Library of Congress Control Number 2014931013
ISBN 978-1-4814-1407-4 (hc)
ISBN 978-1-4814-1406-7 (pbk)
ISBN 978-1-4814-1408-1 (eBook)

CONTENTS

DECEPTION ON THE SET

NARROW ESCAPE

1

FRANK

TRUDGED FORWARD AS BAYPORT BURNED around me. Draped in tattered clothing, I was part of a long line of refugees who looked beaten and hopeless shuffling through the destruction. I felt the heat from flames erupting from storefront windows. Blackened and wrecked vehicles littered the street and sidewalks. The dreary procession veered around a smoldering upturned delivery truck in the middle of the boulevard.

I couldn't believe how my once-beautiful downtown Bayport had been transformed into a postapocalyptic wasteland. Just a week ago, everything was normal. Winslow Pharmacy's huge plate-glass windows were intact instead of in shattered pieces all over the sidewalk. The Dollar Hut was full of shoppers and without flames erupting from the

1

front doors. Sickly sweet instrumental music filled the air in Sal's Diner rather than the buzzing of downed electrical wires. All this mayhem happened in just a short week. Right after *they* came to town.

"Unreal," whispered my brother, Joe, as he lumbered along next to me. His blond hair was almost black, and his face was covered in soot and ash. Like everyone else, Joe wore ripped, threadbare clothing. "I never thought I'd see Bayport like this."

"No kidding," I murmured.

I glanced around at the long line of refugees, many of whom I knew. I spotted some of my classmates and friends, including Eric Watts, Amanda Paul, and Hector Cruz. Even my chemistry teacher, Mr. Watson, wore a torn and stained blue blazer. Mrs. Sally Gertz, owner of Sal's Diner, didn't even look up as she passed her smoking restaurant.

All of a sudden we heard a scream.

Something was happening at the back of the procession. Then, another scream. This one was closer. Everyone picked up the pace. I looked back to see a commotion in the distance. The people at the end of the line were pushing forward, running from something.

"You think we'll see them from here?" asked Joe.

"I don't know," I replied. My stomach knotted with excitement. I knew I was supposed to be frightened, but part of me wanted to see our pursuers, couldn't wait to catch a glimpse of them.

More screams, even closer. The sounds of terror were mixed with primal grunts and growls. Everyone around me moved faster, and I found I had to jog to keep up with the pack. Yet I couldn't help glancing over my shoulder for a glimpse of the creatures terrorizing them. Terrorizing us!

This time I caught flashes of them. Not so far behind us I saw biting teeth and skeletal claws swiping at the crowd. It was a good thing I looked back.

"Oh!" cried Mrs. Gertz as she stumbled and fell to the ground.

I spun around and pushed against the charge of frightened people. All the while the screams and growls grew louder. When I reached Mrs. Gertz, I slipped behind her to shield her from the oncoming crowd. The screams surrounded us, and the rush tripled to a panicked stampede. Grabbing her arms, I helped the woman to her feet.

"Thank you, Frank," she said with a smile. Then her eyes focused on something over my left shoulder. She shrieked and then dashed into the raging river of refugees.

Something clamped onto my left shoulder. I spun around to find myself face-to-decomposing-face with . . . a zombie!

Milky-white eyes stared back at me through pronounced eye sockets. Gray skin stretched over bony cheekbones and pulled away from grinning yellow teeth. Black liquid oozed over its bottom lip as its mouth opened wide, ready to take a bite.

I felt another one grasp my right arm. It jerked me away

just as the first undead creature lunged forward. I stumbled away from the first zombie and spun to confront the second. But luckily, it wasn't a zombie—just Joe.

"You want to be a zombie snack?" asked Joe.

"No way!" I replied.

I stumbled into a run as Joe and I followed the fleeing refugees. A glance back showed a horde of the undead in pursuit. They moved faster than I expected; a few almost kept pace with the escaping mass of Bayport citizens.

This was amazing! Despite the chaos, I couldn't help smiling with delight.

A loud burst of static filled the air. It was followed by a tinny voice amplified over an electronic megaphone.

"And . . . cut!"

MOVIE MAGIC

2

JOE

I **SHOOK MY HEAD AND CHUCKLED. HERE WE WERE,** trapped in the middle of a zombie apocalypse, and my brother was grinning like a little kid on Christmas morning.

"You're supposed to be scared for your life," I told Frank. "They're going to kick you off the movie if you keep breaking character like that."

"I know, but this is just so unreal," Frank said.

I couldn't help but grin as well. I clamped a hand on his shoulder and shook him. "We're in a real Hollywood zombie movie, bro!"

Let me start by saying that the Hardy brothers aren't movie stars in any remote sense of the term. Sure, I played a small part in the school musical last year. I can tell you how everything is up to date in Kansas City (even though the play was called *Oklahoma!*—go figure). But no, acting isn't our thing.

Now, solving mysteries—that's a different story. I suppose we've done a little acting during some undercover work in the past. After all, we've been working cases since we were eight (me) and nine (Frank).

Luckily, there was just made-up movie mayhem here. And even though Frank and I don't always agree, it didn't take much to talk him into spending our spring break working on a zombie movie.

"Okay, Bob, save the fire and smoke," squawked the voice on the megaphone.

"Copy that!" shouted a voice from behind a building. Soon after, the smoke stopped pouring from the rooftops. The sparks ceased inside Sal's Diner. The flames in the other stores and wrecked cars died right down. All part of the movie magic!

The man with the megaphone was Bill Daines, the first assistant director, or first AD. The thin, bearded man aimed the megaphone toward the crowd of extras. "That looked great, everyone. We're going to make a few adjustments and then go again."

"How many times are we going to do the same thing?" asked Hector.

"Welcome to show business," muttered a passing crew member.

Bill pushed through to the center of the extras. "Excuse me, ma'am. Sally, is it?"

"Yes," Mrs. Gertz answered.

"I saw you fall. Are you okay?" he asked.

Mrs. Gertz chuckled and waved him away. "Oh, sure. I just tripped over my own feet."

"Well, it looked great," Bill said. "And if you don't mind doing it again, Josh wants to feature it in the movie."

We all looked over toward "video village." That's what movie people called the group of chairs where the director and producer sat and watched the action on a bunch of video monitors. Josh Biehn, the director, sat in one of the chairs. He pulled a strand of long hair away from his eyes, grinned, and gave Mrs. Gertz a thumbs-up.

She beamed. "I can do it as many times as you want."

Daines laughed. "Just a couple more times." He turned to Frank. "And the way you helped her was good too. Do that again."

"Uh, sure, Mr. Daines," said Frank.

"No misters here, son," he said. "Call me Bill."

After he moved on to some other refugees, Amanda patted Mrs. Gertz on the shoulder. "You're going to be a star, Mrs. Gertz."

"What about me?" I asked. "I saved Frank from becoming a zombie snack."

Eric crossed his arms and stroked his brown goatee. "I

don't know, dude. I wasn't feeling it. I think you should go back to acting school."

"I think he'd be a better zombie," Frank said. "Less acting skill needed."

Amanda smiled. "We'll see tomorrow."

That's right; this movie job was going to get even sweeter! Not only were Frank and I getting paid to be extras in a crowd scene, we would also get to be zombies ourselves! Tomorrow we would report to the makeup department to have our faces cast for the masks that would complete our zombie transformation.

Being a science geek, Frank was excited to learn what chemicals they used to cast our faces and create the makeup. In the past, he had always been the one to make molds of footprints or tire tracks while we were working a case. Now he would get to see what kind of equipment the professionals used. Of course, there was another reason Frank was excited about being in the movie.

Hector glanced around. "Is Chelsea Alexander here yet?"

That was the reason.

"I saw a call sheet," Frank reported. "She's not scheduled to be on set until tomorrow." The call sheet was the daily schedule given to all the crew members.

"You can trust Frank on that intel," I said. "He's had a crush on Chelsea since *Arithme-Trek*."

"Aw, come on," Frank said, turning red.

"What's *Arithme-Trek*?" asked Eric.

"Only where Chelsea Alexander got her start," Amanda replied. "Before the huge movies and even the reality show, when she was little she played a small part on a kids' educational TV show."

"It was kind of like *Star Trek*," I explained. "Except this starship was on a mission to explore strange new math problems."

Eric raised an eyebrow. "You're kidding, right?"

Amanda laughed. "Totally true."

I tapped my chin and looked up. "Now, what was her character's name again?"

"Lieutenant Fraction," Frank mumbled.

Everyone burst into laughter. "Let me guess—she was in charge of . . . fractions?" asked Eric.

"Oh yeah," I agreed. "And Frank nerded out over that show every day after school."

"Hey, I was ten years old," Frank said. "And I liked math!"

"*And* Chelsea Alexander," I added.

A sharp feedback squawk let us know that Bill was about to speak over the megaphone again. "Okay, everyone. Back to one." That signaled all the extras to return to the place where they had started the scene. "We're going again. Bob, let's light it up!"

"Copy that!" a voice shouted. Suddenly smoke billowed from the rooftops and fire erupted from the storefronts and wrecked cars. All the extras moved to their original positions.

We ended up doing the scene only one more time. Just as before, Mrs. Gertz fell and Frank helped her to her feet. This time the zombies didn't make it to us in time, so I didn't get to save him. That was okay with me. I was really looking forward to being a zombie myself soon.

After that scene, they released the extras for the night, but Frank and I decided to stay and watch as they filmed more. The next scene took place atop the roof of Bayport's old savings and loan building. The four-story brick building was one of the oldest in town. It even had one of those metal fire escape stairs bolted to the outside. I guess that's why the director chose that location; from what I could tell, the scene was going to take place on the rickety stairs.

"Excuse me, Bill," I said as the first AD walked by. "What's going to happen here?"

Bill's eyes lit up. "In this scene, a group of survivors climb down the fire escape. As the last one leaves the roof, a zombie lunges at him, and the survivor leaps off the roof and falls four stories down." He pointed to a large air bag being inflated on the sidewalk below. "It's going to be a very cool stunt."

"And we have front-row seats," Frank said, pointing to the inflating air bag.

Several crew members adjusted the white, square-shaped bag. It would stand at over five feet tall when fully inflated. I had seen one on television once, so I knew how it worked. When a stunt person landed in the center of the bag, large flaps on the side would open up, releasing some of the air and breaking the performer's fall.

Frank and I watched as they set up the shot. It seemed like it took forever. When the lights and cameras were finally in place, the stunt performers rehearsed the scene on the roof. Unfortunately, we couldn't hear what was being said from our position. Finally Josh, the director, walked out of the building and sat down in video village.

"Okay, lock it up! Quiet all around!" shouted Bill. "Picture's up!"

The stuntmen and stuntwomen walked to the center of the roof and out of view.

Bill held a walkie-talkie to his mouth. "Roll camera."

"A camera, speed," said the cameraman on the ground.

"B camera, speed," came a voice over the walkie-talkie. It must've been the cameraman on the rooftop.

"And . . . action!" shouted the director.

Atop the roof, the group of survivors came into view. They reached the edge and immediately climbed onto the metal fire escape, their faces contorted into expressions of fear as they descended. The last survivor entered with a zombie close behind. He leaped off the roof and sailed over the edge of the railing, catching the handrail and dangling over the air bag four stories below.

Suddenly the air was filled with the shriek of twisting metal. My heart pounded as I realized the top of the fire escape was coming away from the bricks.

The rickety structure began to fold as the top half leaned away from the side of the building. The group of men and women on the bottom half of the stairs were safe. However, the top portion angled so that it was perpendicular to the brick wall. Now, instead of the stuntman dangling directly over the air bag, he dangled several feet *past* it. The man struggled to cling to the rusty metal railing.

"He's not going to land on the bag," Frank whispered.

My brother was right. If that stuntman lost his hold on the railing, he would tumble straight toward the hard sidewalk below. A fall from that height would kill him. From the way the man fought to keep his grip, it looked as if he didn't have long to live.

CLOSE CALL 3

FRANK

"CUT! CUT!" SHOUTED JOSH. THE DIRECTOR sprang from his chair and ran to the edge of the bag.

"Someone get him down from there!" Bill shouted into the walkie-talkie.

Joe and I rushed forward with the rest of the crew. We all watched helplessly as the stuntman held on for his life.

Joe turned to one of the crew members. "Can we push the air bag under him?"

The blond girl with the clipboard kept staring up at the dangling man. "I don't think you can move it once it's inflated."

"We can try!" I said, running closer to the bag. I grabbed one of the straps and pulled hard. It didn't even budge.

"Come on!" I shouted to anyone who would listen.

Joe was already there, pulling a nearby strap. Soon we were joined by other crew members. With everyone pulling, the large bag began to move.

"We're not going to make it," Joe said, looking up.

I followed his gaze and saw the stuntman's right hand lose its grip. He hung by his left hand while his right hand reached underneath his tattered coat. He pulled out a black strap with a metal oval ring at one end. I recognized the ring at once; it was a carabiner, the same kind of metal clip used in mountain climbing. The man reached up and tried to snap the carabiner onto the metal railing. His face strained as he reached and missed.

I pulled harder at the bag's strap. Everyone seemed to. In fact, by this point, three sides were covered with people. Inch by inch, the giant air bag slid closer to the stuntman's new drop zone.

The man growled as he swung the carabiner one more time. The carabiner struck the railing but didn't attach. His left hand, white and trembling from strain, finally gave out. The stuntman flailed his arms and legs as he fell.

I struggled to pull harder, but the bag didn't budge. For the second time that day, Joe pulled me out of harm's way. We fell backward just as the man hit the bag.

Well, most of him did. His body slammed against the very edge of the bag. Since he didn't land in the center, the bag didn't deflate completely. That plus the odd angle made him bounce off to the side and slam against the hard sidewalk. I cringed as I saw his arm smack against the cement.

We joined the crowd as everyone swooped in around the moaning stuntman.

"Watch your backs!" shouted a voice behind us. "Medics coming through!"

A man and a woman wearing orange jackets pushed through the crowd. Everyone backed off to give them room as they began working on the injured man.

The director rushed in. "Aw, man, Cody. Are you okay?"

The stuntman grimaced with pain and anger. "Does it look like I'm okay?" He grunted as the medics braced his neck and rolled him onto a backboard. "I told you that was a stupid stunt," he growled. "Not enough payoff for the risk."

"I'm so sorry," said Josh. "I didn't think it was that big of a deal. I mean, you've done bigger stunts than that."

"Yeah, well, maybe *you* should've done it, Josh," snarled the stuntman. "Then you could trust your life to some rickety piece of equipment that hasn't been inspected since the 1940s."

The medics lifted the stuntman onto a gurney.

"I thought you were supposed to reinforce it, like I suggested," said Josh.

"We did," replied the injured stuntman. They rolled him through the crowd toward a nearby ambulance.

Josh watched them load him up and pull away. He turned, rubbed his eyes, and gave the watching crew a nervous smile. "I think we're all done for the day," he said. "We'll see you tomorrow."

After the lights had been shut off and equipment packed away, Joe and I headed to my car. "Somewhat stressful first day of show business," I said.

"No kidding," he agreed.

LIFE CAST 4

JOE

DAY TWO ON THE SET WAS MUCH MORE relaxing. I sat in complete darkness while my head and face were massaged by a cool liquid.

Okay, so I wasn't getting a massage in some swanky salon. It just felt as if I was. I sat very still while someone smeared cool, gooey alginate all over my head.

Let me back up. To me, the best thing about being in the movie was that Frank and I got to be actual zombies, with full makeup. To get that zombie look, our heads and faces had to be cast in plaster. In the movie business, they call this a life cast. Once they had a plaster cast of our heads, they could design special zombie makeup that would look like a perfectly fitted mask.

The makeup effects coordinator was a young woman

named Meredith Banks. Though she wasn't much older than Frank and me, she had already worked on some of our favorite horror movies.

"Looking good, man," I heard my brother say. "Your face is like a melting . . . blobby something. Definitely an improvement."

"Now, don't make him laugh," Meredith warned. "This alginate works fast. It'll be firm in another minute."

Since I had to keep my head perfectly still, I just shook a warning finger in my brother's direction.

"All right," said Frank. "No more jabs."

I gave him a thumbs-up of thanks.

"Isn't this the same material dentists use to make molds of teeth?" Frank asked.

"That's right," Meredith replied. "Except this alginate doesn't have the cherry flavor added."

Once the alginate had cured, Meredith and her assistant, Nick, wrapped my head with plaster bandages. The hardened plaster would help the softer alginate keep its shape once it was removed from my head. I couldn't tell by the feel of what they were doing, but I had watched Frank go through the entire process already.

I felt a tap on my shoulder. "We're going to pull Frank's life cast out of the mold," said Meredith. Her voice was a bit muffled through the plaster. "You okay by yourself for a few minutes?"

I gave another thumbs-up.

"Don't go anywhere," said Frank with a chuckle.

I lowered my thumb, leaving just the fist waving in his direction.

I heard the three of them walk away and was left in silence. I had to admit that this part wasn't exactly relaxing. I was completely blind and almost deaf, with the weight of the plaster weighing down my head and shoulders.

And then the unthinkable happened. My nose began to itch. I tried to think of anything to get my mind off it, but nothing was working.

Luckily, I got a distraction when I heard the trailer door open.

"Cody is not happy at all," said a woman's voice. "He blames Josh, you know."

"How can he blame Josh?" asked a second woman. "It was just an accident."

"That's the thing," said the first woman. "Cody thinks that someone sabotaged the—" She stopped midsentence. Then there was silence. I think they just realized that I was sitting there.

"Hello?" asked one of the women. I couldn't tell which one.

I raised a hand and gave a slow wave.

"We're looking for Meredith," said the other woman.

I pointed around and then raised both hands in an *I don't know* kind of gesture. The makeup trailer was sectioned off into several rooms and workstations. If Meredith, Frank, and Nick weren't in plain view, I had no idea where they had gone.

"Thanks," said the first woman. "We'll check back later."

I heard the trailer door shut. Once again, there was only silence. However, this time I had plenty to keep my mind occupied. I hadn't recognized either of the women's voices, but I definitely recognized the names they had mentioned. Josh was Josh Biehn, the director. The night before, he had called the stuntman who almost fell Cody. So, according to the voices I heard, the stuntman didn't think that the falling fire escape was an accident.

My thoughts were interrupted by the sound of a distant door opening and approaching footsteps.

"He didn't wander off," joked Frank. "Right where we left him."

"Let's get you out of there," said Meredith.

She pulled the mold off my head in two halves. I leaned forward as she removed the front part. As soon as it was gone, I reached up and scratched the tip of my nose.

I moaned. "Oh yeah! That's the stuff."

Meredith laughed. "Don't worry. You're not the first person to get an itchy nose."

After she and Nick removed the back half of the mold, I caught a glimpse of myself in the mirror. My eyebrows were slicked down with petroleum jelly to keep the alginate from sticking to them. To protect the rest of my hair, I wore a skin wig. I looked like a bald alien clone or something.

Meredith leaned in beside me and caught my eye in the mirror. Her short brown hair was pulled back into a ponytail. "All good?" she asked.

"Oh yeah," I replied. "I just forgot how weird I looked."

"You think that's weird? Check this out!" said Frank. He squatted near a table and placed an arm around a life-size bust of himself.

"Hey, I'm seeing double," I remarked.

"Pretty cool, huh?" he asked.

As Meredith and Nick carried away the molds from my head, I stood and leaned closer to Frank.

"You think that's cool?" I asked. "I think I just stumbled onto a mystery."

FIRST ENCOUNTERS

5

FRANK

"IT COULD'VE JUST BEEN AN ACCIDENT," I NOTED as we left the makeup trailer.

"But what if it wasn't?" Joe's eyes lit up. "We could have ourselves a real mystery here."

Joe and I made our way past the long line of semi-trailers parked along Cheshire Avenue. Like the makeup trailer, each one was outfitted for a different movie department. There was the camera trailer, the special effects trailer, and the trailer for grips and electric (the department in charge of all the lights and light stands). The usually quiet residential street looked like a truck stop.

I came to a halt. "Look, you talked me into this and now you want to ruin it by nosing around for a mystery that may or may not exist." I shook my head. "Can't you just be happy to be in a cool zombie movie?"

"Dude, I'm *thrilled* to be in a cool zombie movie." Joe glanced around. "I'm just saying . . . we're not working until tomorrow. What's the harm in being curious?"

I tightened my lips. "Plenty."

Look, nobody likes an unsolved mystery more than me. Our dad is a retired private investigator, so it's in our blood. That and the fact that we've always managed to solve cases had always bought us a little pull with a few of the town's police officers, even Chief Gomez. But now the guy in charge was Chief Olaf. Former *Detective* Olaf had never liked us and had always been resentful when we closed cases that he couldn't solve. He was never happy to catch us looking for a mystery on our own.

Joe pointed to a trailer up ahead. "Let's just go say hello to the stunt department. What do you say?"

"Joe . . . ," I began, but he was already walking toward the long trailer.

I caught up to him just as he reached the stunt trailer. The back doors were open, revealing a rig full of large pads of every shape and size. There was personal safety gear like helmets, elbow pads, and kneepads. Tons of harnesses, ropes, and carabiners hung from the walls. Near the open doors, a tall, thin guy not much older than us used a long stick to stir a solution in a white bucket.

"How's it going?" asked Joe. "I'm Joe and this is my brother, Frank." He gave a short bow. "And we'll be your zombies today. Or tomorrow, at least."

The man laughed and extended a hand. "I'm Chase."

"Actually, we just wanted to see how that stuntman was doing," said Joe. "From last night? I think his name was Cody."

"Cody Langstrom," said Chase. "He's actually the stunt coordinator for the show. And he's fine."

"Didn't he break his arm?" I asked.

"We thought so," replied Chase. "But he just strained it. They gave him the once-over at the hospital last night. Other than a few bruises, he checked out just fine. He should be back any time now." He went back to stirring the liquid in the bucket.

Now that we were closer, I could see that the liquid was clear but very thick, almost like syrup.

"What's that?" I asked, pointing at the bucket. "If you don't mind me asking."

"Not at all." The man pulled the stick out, and clear slime oozed off the tip. "I'm making up another batch of stunt gel."

"Stunt gel?" asked Joe.

"Yeah, we put this stuff on us when we do a fire gag." Chase stirred some more. "Think of it as water that doesn't run off. This gel keeps a thin layer of moisture all over our bodies. That way when we're in a fire, we don't turn into crispy critters."

"Very cool," said Joe.

"Literally," said Chase. "Give it a try."

Joe and I leaned in and dipped our fingers into the bucket. The stuff was slimy and oozed off our fingertips like runny egg whites. But after a moment, my fingers felt cool. It seemed to work the same way sweat cools our bodies. But this stuff didn't evaporate (or stink, for that matter).

"What is it made of?" I asked.

Before Chase could answer, a truck pulled to a stop beside the trailer. Cody Langstrom stepped out from behind the passenger seat, waving to the driver. Cody's right arm was in a sling.

"There he is," said Chase. "No worse for wear?"

"I'm all right," growled Cody. "I'm supposed to wear this stupid thing for a few days." He nodded to the sling.

"This is Frank and Joe," said Chase. "A couple of our zombies."

"We will be tomorrow," I added. "We just got our life casts made."

"I can see that," said Langstrom. He reached up and scratched his left ear.

I was about ask how he knew, but I was interrupted by my brother diving right in, headfirst as usual.

"Sorry about your accident," he put in. "What happened?"

Langstrom shook his head. "Someone is not a fan of stunts, me, or this movie. That's what happened."

There it was. Right out in the open. "Sabotage?" I asked.

Cody nodded. "That's what I think."

"Any idea who did it?" asked Joe.

"No," Cody replied. He eyed Joe suspiciously. "Why do you ask?"

"Maybe we can help find out," said Joe. "We're pretty good at—"

I cut him off. "What he means is that we'll let you know if we hear anything." I ushered Joe away from the trailer. "But we'll let you get back to work now."

When we were several yards away, Joe stopped walking. "What was up with that?" he asked. "You never turn down a good mystery."

I held up a finger. "One. It may, just *may* be a mystery." I held up a second finger. "Two. Chief Olaf already doesn't like us snooping around when people ask us for help. What do you think he'd do if we started investigating on our own?" Joe opened his mouth to reply, but I held up a third finger. "And three . . . it could get us kicked off the only movie we've ever had a chance to be a part of."

Joe threw up his hands. "Okay, okay. Sheesh!" He backed away. "No investigating. Got it." Then he grinned. "Still going to keep my ear to the ground, though. You never know." He turned and continued to walk beside the long row of trailers.

I sighed and followed him. It was the best I could hope for, really. Joe could never turn down a mystery. And he was right; I usually couldn't either. Actually, I was more than a little intrigued about the sabotaged stunt. I just didn't want to blow this opportunity. We were learning so much about the film industry and how movies were made. Plus, to be completely honest, I didn't want to ruin my chances of meeting Chelsea Alexander.

Little did I know, my wish was about to come true. As Joe and I walked past the catering trailer, we almost ran into three girls coming around the side. One of the girls was Chelsea herself. Joe and I skidded to a stop, just barely keeping from plowing them over.

"Whoa!" said Joe.

Okay, I know this sounds dumb, but when I saw Chelsea in person, I felt as if I was nine years old again. My stomach tightened into that familiar knot, the same one I had felt when I watched her show after school. Her once-long curly brown hair was now short and straight. She was taller, of course, but she still had those same pale-green eyes. Back then I had had one powerful crush. And when I saw her it was as if it had never gone away.

Joe didn't seem to be as awestruck as I was. He thrust out a hand. "Hi. I'm Joe and this is my brother, Frank."

Chelsea's friends checked their phones while Chelsea reached into her purse. "Do you two want autographs?"

"No," Joe replied. "I mean, we're in the movie too." He glanced at me and smiled. "We're going to be zombies."

Chelsea smiled. "That's great." She looked at me, obviously expecting me to say something. I opened my mouth to agree with Joe, but all I could get out was an "uh-huh."

Joe grinned. He was clearly enjoying this way too much. When he opened his mouth to speak, I knew what he was going to say. My eyes widened in horror, but it was too late.

"Frank has been a mega-fan of yours since *Arithme-Trek*," he announced.

"Oh yeah?" she asked. She smiled and took a step closer. "Do you like math?"

This time I was able to smooth-talk my way into almost two words. "Uh . . . yeah."

She took another step closer as my heart hammered in my chest. "I see you've already had your life casts made."

I opened my mouth to reply, but nothing came out. How did everyone seem to know that?

She reached a hand toward my face, and I swear, my heart stopped beating altogether. Then she lightly brushed my left ear. She pulled her finger away, and it had a white smudge on the tip.

"Alginate," she said. "I've seen my share of this stuff, believe me."

It's a scientific fact that my heart really hadn't stopped. But at that moment, I was so embarrassed that I wish it had.

DECOMPOSING 6

JOE

"STILL NOT TALKING TO ME?" I ASKED Frank. My brother didn't answer. Instead he stared forward as Meredith slowly turned him into a zombie.

It had been like that for the rest of the day yesterday. I thought that after a good night's sleep Frank would finally accept my apology. I really hadn't noticed the alginate on his ear. And I was just trying to help him break the ice with Chelsea. But I continued to get the silent treatment all through breakfast and during the drive to the makeup trailer.

"You guys have a fight?" Meredith asked, not taking her eyes off her work.

Frank shot me a look that meant I had better keep my mouth shut.

I shrugged. "No big deal." I pointed to Frank's half-zombified face. "So how many of those pieces do we have to wear?"

"You guys have pretty simple masks," Meredith replied. She glanced up and smiled. "Since you're not the stars of the show"—she pulled another floppy piece of foam from a nearby table—"your makeup consists of just five prosthetic pieces."

It was fascinating to watch Meredith turn Frank into one of the undead. After she had cast our heads, Nick had taken clay and sculpted zombie faces over our plaster faces. Then he had taken a mold of our completed zombie faces. Once that mold was ready, the clay was removed. Now, if you put both molds together, there would be an empty space where the zombie-face-shaped clay had been. Nick used this empty space to create the foam makeup pieces that would eventually get applied to our real faces. I know all this because Frank had been fascinated and had asked a million questions. Apparently, his silent treatment didn't extend to everyone else.

Meredith attached a foam piece to Frank's chin. This new zombie chin was made to look as if some of the skin was gone, with a piece of jawbone showing—way gross but way cool. She had also applied foam pieces to Frank's forehead, one on each eye and cheek, another over his nose and upper lip, and finally, one over his chin and lower lip.

"We cut the mask into all these pieces so it will be able to move with his face," Meredith explained. "That way he can still make different expressions."

Even though the seams weren't painted yet, I could see how Frank was going to look like a creepy zombie. Small flaps of what was supposed to be dried skin peeled away from his forehead. The rest of the mask made it look as if his skin was stretched tightly over his skull. He had sharp cheekbones and pronounced eye sockets. Just like his chin, some of the skin was made to look as if it was missing, so parts of his skull jutted through.

"I hope my makeup looks as sick as that," I said.

"Don't worry. It will," Meredith assured me.

Frank glanced over at me. "Anything will be an improvement." He gave half a grin that wouldn't have looked so creepy if he wasn't covered in zombie makeup.

So just like that, our fight was over. Like any brothers, Frank and I got into the occasional tiff, but luckily, we never stayed angry with each other for very long.

"All right," said Meredith. "Let's get you over to Nick so he can touch up those seams and add your wig."

Meredith led Frank away to another room in the large trailer. When she returned, she had me sit in the makeup chair. She threw an apron over my shoulders just as she had done with Frank.

"Remember what I told your brother," warned Meredith. "It's going to itch in some places as I apply the makeup. Resist the urge to scratch."

"This time I came prepared," I said as I dug my MP3 player out of my pocket. "Something to take my mind off everything."

"Good idea," agreed Meredith.

I popped in my earbuds and played some tunes as Meredith began applying the foam prosthetic pieces to my face. I closed my eyes and tried to relax. Every now and then as she applied adhesive to my face, part of my skin would begin to itch, particularly around my nose and eyes. I concentrated on the music until the sensation went away.

I must've really zoned out. I hadn't even noticed that the album on my MP3 player had finished playing. I also hadn't noticed that Chelsea had entered the trailer. I still had my eyes closed, but there was no mistaking her voice.

"And go by the caterer trailer and find out what's for lunch," Chelsea instructed. "If it's anything like yesterday, I'm going to send you out again."

"There's not much tofu in this town," said another girl's voice. It must've been Chelsea's assistant. "But I'll keep looking."

A smiled touched my lips. Whoever she was, she was right. The customers at Sal's Diner and the Meet Locker weren't exactly tofu types.

Chelsea sighed. "I'll be glad when this movie is over. I don't think Josh knows what he's doing."

"Well, this is the first movie he's written and directed," Meredith explained. She dabbed some more adhesive on my chin. "I think he's doing all right, considering."

"What was he before?" asked Chelsea. "A stuntman or something?"

"That's what I heard," said Meredith.

"That's why there are so many stunts in this movie," said Chelsea's assistant.

"Not very good ones, according to Cody," added Chelsea. "In fact, I heard that Cody and Josh—" Her voice cut off as I heard approaching footsteps.

Meredith nudged my arm. "You can open your eyes now." She chuckled. "And sorry to hear about your brother's passing."

Upon opening my eyes, I noticed that Frank looked as if he had returned from the dead—a full-fledged zombie. The makeup was incredible; his skin really looked as if it was dried and stretched across his skull. Frank's hands were now painted to match his face—but that wasn't the best part. He wore contacts that made his eyes look milky white. My older brother grinned, revealing yellow rotting teeth.

"Very nice!" I said.

Frank's grin vanished when his eyes cut over to Chelsea. I followed his gaze to see that another makeup artist was busy applying a realistic cut to her forehead.

"Wow," said Chelsea. "That . . . looks really creepy." She gave a small wave. "Hi. I'm Chelsea."

"Actually, you already met us yesterday," I explained. "I'm Joe and this is my decomposing brother, Frank."

Recognition showed on Chelsea's face. "Oh yeah."

Frank must've gained more confidence hiding behind the mask. This time he didn't choke. He stepped forward and extended a hand to Chelsea.

Now, I don't know what Frank tried to say to her. But whatever it was, it came out sounding like "Grape-dosheekjubejegeng." His milky eyes widened as he snapped his mouth shut. He twisted his mouth and tried again. "Crage joob meek kook magain." Unfortunately, speaking slowly didn't seem to help.

Chelsea and her assistant exchanged a glance before cracking up.

Meredith chuckled. "It takes some practice to speak with the mouth prosthetics," she explained. "Don't worry. You'll get it."

"Luckily, I think we just have to groan a lot," I said.

Even through all the zombie makeup, I could tell that Frank was *way* embarrassed—again.

WINDFALL 7

FRANK

KAY, A LITTLE SLOWER," HUGO ORDERED. "And a little stiffer, too. Remember, rigor mortis has set in for most of you."

I felt as if we were in the Michael Jackson "Thriller" video. Joe and I stood among a group of twenty zombies. Hugo, the second AD, was instructing everyone on how to properly act like zombies. He had a couple of zombies cock their heads to one side, as if their necks were broken. He had others limp and hobble as if their legs had been broken. Joe and I were in a group that just shuffled and moaned a lot. The entire "zombie university," as Hugo had called it, was surreal.

Actually, I was thrilled to be wearing the heavy makeup. Even though it had happened a couple of hours ago, I suspected that my face was still red with embarrassment. I couldn't believe that I had met Chelsea Alexander twice and both times had made a fool of myself. The zombie lessons were a nice distraction.

Joe spat his fake teeth into his hand and raised it. "I thought we were going to be fast zombies," he said. "Like in *World War Z* or *28 Days Later.*" He glanced around. "You have us moving more like *Night of the Living Dead* zombies."

"Good point," said Hugo. "Josh wants there to be a variety. If you're a fresh zombie, you can move faster," he explained. "If you have a broken limb or look as if you crawled out of a grave, we're going to assume that rigor has set in and you move slowly."

Joe spread his arms wide. "Makes perfect sense, actually."

I took out my teeth and raised a hand. "Excuse me."

Hugo pointed at me. "Yes, that zombie there has a question?"

"I don't have a question, really," I said. "But I wanted to point out that rigor mortis is a temporary condition. A corpse's muscles go through rigor between four to six hours after death. Then, after seventy-two hours, depending on the temperature and a few other factors, decomposition begins to break down the tissue and the stiffness goes away. This fact often helps investigators determine the approximate time of death."

I smiled and looked at Joe for confirmation but instead

saw him do a face palm. You don't see a zombie do that every day.

Hugo stared at me blankly.

I shrugged. "It's a scientific fact."

Hugo finally laughed. "Well, since this is just a movie, we're going to use a little creative license, okay?"

The rest of the zombies laughed. Joe leaned closer. "Scientifically, corpses don't get up and start walking around, either," he whispered.

I shook my head. "I was just trying to be helpful."

After all of us zombies learned to shamble, moan, and groan correctly, we were sent to a large tent full of folding chairs and bad coffee. We waited there for almost two hours. It was pretty surreal sitting around with a bunch of zombies listening to MP3 players, texting, and taking pictures of one another.

Finally Hugo stepped into the tent. "Okay, zombies. We're ready for you."

He led us a block away to Wilson Avenue. The set for this scene was in front of Mike's Movies & Music. Just like the stores on Main Street, Mike's was dressed to look as if it had been looted and half-destroyed. The only difference was that the formerly small shop now looked like a two-story building.

"Looks like Mike's got an upgrade," Joe announced.

"Okay, zombies, gather round," ordered Hugo. Once we surrounded him, he pointed to the camera crew on the other side of the street. "We'll be shooting from over there. The scene has three survivors making their way down this street. When they get in front of this building, all the zombies are going to come out and make a grab for them." He began pointing to different zombies. "You three, hide behind that wrecked truck. You hide behind that Dumpster." He pointed to Joe and me. "You two hide behind the building."

When Joe and I arrived behind Mike's, I could see that a large flat facade had been installed over the entrance. It looked as if it was made from plywood and had long boards propping it up. From the front, however, the facade simply looked like a large brick building.

We came back outside to watch as the survivors met the director in the middle of the street. I could tell who they were by their tattered clothing and the cuts, bruises, and scrapes applied to their faces. I could also make out that one of the survivors was none other than Chelsea Alexander.

"Dude, our first scene with Chelsea," said Joe.

"I understood everything you just said," I told him.

"Yeah?" asked Joe.

"That means it's time to put in our fake teeth," I explained.

"Oh yeah," said Joe.

We both dug our sets of teeth from our pockets and popped them into our mouths. They weren't comfortable, but they certainly completed our decomposing personas.

I watched as Josh spoke to the actors. That's when I vowed not to talk to Chelsea Alexander ever again. I had already made a fool of myself twice; I wasn't going for number three.

"Okay, rehearsal's up," Bill Daines shouted. "We'll cue the survivors on 'action,' and I'll give a second cue for the zombies. First positions, everyone."

Joe and I ducked back around the corner of Mike's revamped store. Joe turned to me, and if it wasn't for the milky contacts he wore, I knew I would've seen a gleam in his eyes.

"It's showtime," he said. Or that's what I think he said. With the fake teeth in his mouth, it sounded more like, "This thowthime."

"Action!" shouted Josh.

I could hear Chelsea and the others speaking but I couldn't make out what they said. Then, after a lull in the conversation, we heard from Bill.

"Zombies!"

That was our cue. We shuffled out from behind Mike's. The scene was alive with wisps of smoke and flames erupting from debris on the ground. It looked as if the special effects team was rehearsing as well.

Joe and I shambled aimlessly until we pretended to notice the survivors. Just as we'd been taught in zombie university, we quickened our pace and moved toward them. We groaned as we pretended to yearn for a tasty snack. Chelsea screamed as zombies closed in around her. The survivors tried to escape, but there were undead moving in from every direction.

"They're everywhere!" Chelsea cried. Her eyes widened with fright. "What do we do?"

"This way!" bellowed the man next to her. He led the other two to a burned-out SUV in the middle of the street. They clambered up the hood and stood on the roof.

The rest of us zombies closed in. We encircled the car and reached for the survivors. Chelsea screamed again as one of the zombies got too close.

"And . . . cut!" shouted Josh. "Great job, you guys. Let's shoot this thing!"

"Okay, back to one," shouted Bill.

Chelsea and the other two survivors climbed down from the car, and the zombies moved back to their starting positions.

Bill held a radio to his mouth. "Hey, Bob. Can your people get us a little more smoke? The wind is picking up."

"More smoke. Copy that," replied Bob's voice on the radio.

I hadn't noticed, but the wind *was* getting stronger. The flaming debris flickered, and the smoke turned from a fog to tendrils weaving down the street. Even the facade on Mike's Movies & Music was swaying a bit.

Joe and I returned to our places and waited for our cue.

"Lock it up!" yelled Bill. "Picture's up. Roll camera."

"Speed!" yelled the cameraman.

"Action!" shouted Josh.

While Chelsea and the other survivors delivered their

lines, I heard the facade knocking against the building. I looked up and at first glance noticed it didn't seem so structurally sound. I thought I saw something strange, but before I could investigate further . . .

"Zombies!" shouted Bill.

As before, we shambled out and pretended to hunger for human flesh. Just as we had rehearsed, we cornered the survivors atop the burned-out SUV.

"Cut!"

After that take, Josh came out to talk to the survivors as we zombies returned to our first positions. Joe and I didn't speak; it was practically useless with the prosthetic teeth in our mouths. Instead I turned my attention to what I thought I'd seen earlier.

The fake storefront wasn't physically attached to the front of the store. Instead it was supported by several long boards reaching to the top of the facade. The boards angled away from the wall and toward the ground. There, they met other boards that were flat on the ground and attached to the bottom of the facade. Together they formed a big triangle, with heavy sandbags holding the whole thing down. The sandbags were in place, but the fake wall still swayed in the wind.

"And . . . action!" came Josh's voice from the street.

I moved closer to one of the braces and noticed holes where the two long boards had been screwed together where they met. I say *had been* because they were no longer attached. The sandbag sat on the bottom board, but the top board just slapped against the bottom as the wind picked up. There was a small pile of screws on the ground next to the wood.

"Zombies!" came Bill's voice.

Joe shuffled out into the street, but I stayed behind. I felt compelled to examine the other braces. Just as I feared, each one of them had been disassembled, and each had a small pile of screws sitting next to it. The wind ruffled my clothes, and I glanced up at the facade, which swayed even more. One good gust would blow it over, and it would land on anyone who happened to be in the street at the time. Right now that meant almost everyone in this scene.

I dashed out from behind the building, frantically waving my arms. "The storefront set piece is going to fall!" I shouted. Unfortunately, with a mouth full of plastic teeth, all that came out was, "Dashettwisdondoonfrawl!"

None of the zombies or survivors paid attention to me. The zombies continued to clamber for the three people huddled on the SUV roof.

"Dashettwisdondoonfrawl!" This time I pointed to the swaying facade as I shouted.

Joe turned and saw where I pointed. He immediately shook the shoulder of the nearest zombie to get his attention. Staying in character, the zombie shrugged him off and went back to reaching for the survivors.

I looked up and saw the tall set piece swaying even more. It was definitely coming down.

"Cut! Cut!" shouted Josh. He marched onto the set. "What's going on?"

I spat out my fake teeth. "Everybody out!" I ordered. "The storefront is going to fall!" I raced toward the group, shoving as many people in the right direction as possible. Joe was doing the same.

As the survivors scrambled off the car a gust of wind blew through. Smoke snaked over the scene as the sound of creaking wood filled the air.

The set piece was on its way down.

By this time, Joe and I had cleared the area of zombies. Only the survivors remained.

"Come on!" I shouted, running toward the car. The two men hopped off the hood, but Chelsea stayed, frozen in place with fear. I shot up at her, threw an arm around her waist, and jerked her off the hood. The four of us ran for safety just as the large facade slammed against the SUV, smashing the roof and shattering glass everywhere.

MISTAKEN IDENTITY

8

JOE

FRANK AND I SAT ON THE CURB WATCHING as Chief Olaf and a few officers took statements from everyone. Though it's unusual for a police chief to be assisting in an investigation, I wasn't surprised to see him out there. Knowing Chief Olaf, he probably jumped at the chance to hobnob with the stars (and get the Bayport police some free publicity in the process).

Frank scratched his face for the twentieth time. He'd been doing it ever since Nick had removed our makeup.

"Dude, you're going to leave a red mark," I warned. "What will Chelsea think the next time she sees her big hero?"

"I'm not her big hero," denied Frank. He reached up to scratch again but then caught himself and stopped.

I laughed. "Right."

We watched as the chief moved on to Bob Trevino, the special effects coordinator. The short, dark-haired man was the person called upon whenever a scene needed more smoke, fire, or sparks.

Bob was very animated as he spoke. He even pointed in our direction a couple of times. I guessed he was pointing out that Frank was the one who had discovered the loose set piece. A police officer stood nearby, taking careful notes.

"So what do you think?" I asked Frank. "Have you solved the case of the cinematic saboteur?"

Frank sighed. "Look, do I think there's a mystery here?" he asked. "Yes. And are we working the case? No."

"Speak for yourself," I said. Even though I had been initially excited about the mystery, it had honestly slipped my mind amid the excitement of being in the movie.

"No," insisted Frank. "We're not working on this case. That's the truth, and that's exactly what we'll tell Chief Olaf when he asks."

I sighed. "And you know he's going to ask."

"You *know* he is," agreed Frank.

As Bob Trevino walked away from Chief Olaf and the other officer, he cast another look toward us. The chief ambled over to us.

"Hello, Hardys," he greeted us.

"Hi, Chief Olaf," we replied, almost in unison.

The chief turned to Frank. "I hear you had a busy day."

"I just tried to help," said Frank. "It was no big deal."

"Only if saving the life of the star of the movie isn't considered a big deal," I said.

The chief glanced at me. "Right." He returned his gaze to Frank. "Quite the hero."

I didn't get why he was picking on Frank. I tried to change the subject. "And before you ask, Chief, we are not, I repeat *not* trying to solve this case."

"You're not, are you?" he asked.

I shook my head. "No, sir. We're just playing a couple of zombies in a cool horror movie."

"Not thinking about the recent events," the chief confirmed.

"Not at all," Frank agreed.

The chief took a deep breath. "Well, that's good. Because we may have this one solved already."

I was shocked. "Really?" I asked. Usually we beat Olaf to the punch, not the other way around.

"That's right," the chief replied. "We even have an eyewitness to the latest incident."

Frank and I glanced at each other. "Well, that's great," said Frank.

The chief narrowed his eyes at Frank. "You think it's great, do you? Can you tell me your whereabouts between noon and two o'clock this afternoon?"

Frank's mouth fell open. He was speechless. It sounded as if Chief Olaf suspected my brother.

"Why do you ask?" I asked.

He kept his eyes on Frank. "Just answer the question, son."

"Uh . . . ," Frank began. "I was in the makeup trailer. Getting my zombie makeup applied."

"Is that right?" asked the chief, eyeing Frank suspiciously.

"It's true," I confirmed. "He was with me the entire time."

"You saw him the *entire* time?" asked the chief.

"Yeah," I replied. "Except when he went to get his wig put on." My lips slammed shut, but the damage was done. "He wasn't gone that long, though."

"And I was with Nick, one of the makeup artists, during that part," Frank added. "You can ask him."

"Oh, I will." The chief nodded to the nearby police officer, who scribbled something in his notepad.

"Why do you want to know where Frank was?" I asked.

The chief grinned. "Remember that eyewitness I told you about? Well, he named Frank as the saboteur. Says he saw him near Mike's, fiddling with the building's facade."

"No way!" I exclaimed.

"It's not true!" protested Frank.

The chief didn't reply. I could tell that he was studying our faces to see if we were lying.

"Look, you know me, Chief," said Frank. "I wouldn't do anything like that!"

"You wouldn't, huh?" The chief turned to me. "Maybe if there wasn't a mystery, you'd want to create one of your very own. One you could solve? Then you could be the big hero, save the leading lady and all that."

"That's crazy," I said. "Who is this eyewitness, anyway?"

"I don't think that's hard to figure out," Frank said, turning to Chief Olaf. "It's Bob Trevino, isn't it?"

The chief nodded almost imperceptibly. "Not that that's any of your concern." He turned to the nearby officer. "Let's find this Nick and ask him a few questions."

They marched away, leaving my brother and me dumbfounded.

I rounded on Frank. "Now do you think this mystery is worth solving?"

"It's insane is what it is," muttered Frank. "I would never do anything like that."

I clamped a hand on Frank's shoulder. "I know that and you know that. But this 'eyewitness' doesn't know that. What do you say we do just . . . a smidgen of investigating?"

"What do you mean?" asked Frank, apparently still shaken by the accusation.

"Follow me," I said, leading the way. "Let's question Trevino ourselves."

We hiked back to Cheshire Avenue, where the production trailers were set up, careful not to be spotted by Chief Olaf as we passed the makeup trailer. We jogged all the way down the street until we found the special effects trailer. You couldn't miss it; it was the only trailer surrounded by smoke. As we approached, we saw that the "smoke" wasn't smoke at all, but dust. A figure dressed in brown coveralls stood in the center of the dust cloud, wielding a loud power tool. Behind him, a framed white board was covered with crisscrossed lines.

"Excuse me!" I shouted over the whine of the motor.

The figure turned, and the power tool spun down. As the dust settled, we saw that the young man was one of the special effects technicians. He wore goggles and a particle mask and was covered with chalky dust. The power tool was a large circular saw.

"Hi," said Frank. "We were wondering if we could speak with—"

I pointed to the framed white board. "What exactly are you doing?"

The technician pointed to his work. "This is for a scene where one of the stunt performers bursts through a wall," he explained. "We score the Sheetrock by sawing it almost completely through. That way it'll be easier to break."

Bob Trevino stepped out of the trailer doors. "Hey, Chuck. When you're done with that—" The man's face hardened when he saw us. "What do you two want?"

"We want to know why you told the police chief that I sabotaged that set," growled Frank.

Mr. Trevino rolled his eyes. "Oh, I don't know . . . because I saw you messing with it earlier today?"

"But I wasn't," protested Frank. "You have the wrong guy."

The man took a step forward, eyes flashing. "I know what

I saw. *Who* I saw." He aimed a finger at Frank's chest. "I saw *you* behind the set with a screw gun. I had seen you around, so I assumed you were with the construction department. I didn't think anything of it at the time. But after the set piece fell and I heard that you warned everyone, I put two and two together."

I raised my hands. "Sir, I know for a fact that my brother wasn't anywhere near where you saw him. He was in the makeup trailer with me." I pointed back to the long line of trailers. "The police are confirming his alibi as we speak."

Trevino tightened his lips and looked us both over. Finally he said, "If it wasn't you, then it was your twin brother."

"I'm his only brother," I said. "And as you can clearly see, he's not nearly as good-looking."

"Hey," said Frank.

I shrugged. "Trying to defuse the tension."

"Look, guys." Trevino sighed and shook his head. "I'm just telling you what I saw."

DEAD RUN

9

FRANK

I STEPPED OUT OF THE MAKEUP TRAILER WEARING a three-piece suit, Italian leather shoes, and a gold watch. I caught a few puzzled looks from people as I strolled down the street. Of course, they didn't stare because of my fancy clothes. They stared at the decomposing skin stretched over my bony skull.

Did I mention my suit was tattered, my shoes were scuffed, and the gold watch encircled my rotting wrist? That's right, I was a zombie once again. But today I played a higher class of living dead.

I was also a little sleepy, since the police had kept everyone late the night before. They didn't want anyone leaving until they questioned the entire crew. Lucky for me, Chief Olaf spoke to Nick, who confirmed my alibi. I felt a little better, but I still didn't understand why Bob Trevino believed I was the saboteur. Joe had speculated that Bob himself was the culprit and was trying to frame me in order to throw the police off the scent. I wasn't so sure.

Hugo met me halfway between the trailer and the set. "Looking good, Frank," he said. Then he held a radio to his mouth. "I have our zombie and we're flying in."

This morning the set was located in the alley behind Sal's Diner. The crew was there with all lights, stands, video village, and craft service—that's what they called the snack table. Unfortunately, craft service was off-limits for me. Zombie teeth make chewing difficult.

Hugo led me to the center of the alley, where the crew adjusted a couple of small lights and focused the camera on me. I was used to waiting while working on this movie, but today I didn't have to wait very long before Chelsea Alexander joined me on set.

Chelsea looked me in the eye, trying to recognize me. "You're the guy from yesterday, right? Fred?"

"Frank," I managed to say with my zombie teeth.

"Oh, okay. Frank," she said. "I just want to thank you for saving me."

I opened my mouth to speak but stopped myself. I held up a finger and then turned my back to her as I removed my prosthetic teeth. The only thing more gross than spitting out something in front of a girl was being a zombie and spitting out your teeth in front of a girl.

I turned back to her. "It was no big deal," I said, trying hard to compose myself. Even though I'd vowed not to speak to her again for fear of embarrassment, so far I was doing okay.

"It was too a big deal," said Chelsea. "I think you saved my life."

Now I was embarrassed for a different reason. Again, I was glad that she couldn't see my face, which I'm sure was beet red.

I scratched the back of my head. "Us zombies were trying to grab you anyway," I explained. "I was just method acting."

Chelsea laughed, and I felt relief wash over me. I was actually having a conversation with Chelsea Alexander and *not* making a fool of myself. I'd even made her laugh. Cool.

"Okay, are you ready, Chelsea?" asked Josh as he marched over.

"I'm ready," she replied.

Josh pointed down the alley. "For this scene, you're going to run down the alley while this zombie chases after you." He patted my shoulder. "Chelsea, I want you to try the first two doors on the left. They'll be locked. But then I want you to duck into the last door on the right. It'll be open."

"Got it," said Chelsea.

"And you," Josh said to me. "Just be a zombie. Almost catch her when she's at the second door."

"Yes, sir," I said.

Josh walked back to video village. Bill stepped forward

and addressed the crew. "Picture's up! No rehearsal. Let's shoot this one."

Once everyone was in place, Josh yelled, "Action!"

Chelsea screamed as she ran down the alley. I shambled after her, doing my best stiff-legged zombie impression. Chelsea looked over her shoulder at me, her eyes wide with terror, and screamed. She was good; I almost stopped chasing her for a second. But then I snapped out of it and picked up the pace when she hit the first door. She jerked the knob back and forth, but it didn't open. She dashed away from my reaching arms and made for the second door. As promised, it was locked. This time, I clutched at her jacket. Chelsea screamed as she jerked it from my grip.

When she hit the third door, I was right behind her. She jerked it open and ducked inside. I arrived just as the door slammed in my face. I groaned and beat the door with my fists.

"And . . . cut!" shouted Josh.

I thought it looked like a cool scene, though I wasn't sure how it would play out in the rest of the movie. Neither Joe nor I had read the screenplay—movie extras didn't get copies of the script.

Josh jogged over. "Everything looked great, you guys. I just want to add one thing." He turned to me. "I want you to grab her jacket just as before. But this time, don't let go."

"Okay," I said.

"And, Chelsea . . . really try to break free," Josh instructed. "If you have to rip the jacket or take it off altogether, go ahead. We have more just like it."

"Sure thing, Josh," she said. Josh walked away, and she rolled her eyes when she turned back to me. I laughed politely, but I didn't understand what the big deal was. I'm no director, but Josh's instructions sounded good to me.

As we moved back to our first positions, I noticed Joe standing off to the side. He was wearing brown overalls, so I guess he had been helping Meredith with some messy chemicals in the makeup trailer. He must've just stepped away to check out my big scene. I gave him a wave, but he didn't wave back, which was weird because he seemed to be looking right at me.

"And . . . action!" shouted Josh.

Chelsea ran from me as before, but this time I clung to her jacket as Josh had instructed. But I wasn't ready for how hard she would fight back, and she quickly jerked it from my grasp. She was safe behind the doorway after that.

"Okay, let's try it again," said Josh. "And this time hold on and don't let go."

"Will do," I told him.

I looked over to where Joe had been, but he was gone. I scanned the crew and spotted my brother standing next to a huge movie light on a lowered crane. The light was on a large stand inside the crane's bucket. Long yellow straps extended from the bucket to the light itself. There were four of them, and they seemed to be all that was keeping the light from tipping out of the basket.

That's when I noticed that Joe wasn't merely standing by the light; he was examining the yellow straps. I wondered what he was up to. Had he found a lead in the case?

"And . . . action!" shouted Josh.

Chelsea and I went through the scene again. This time, however, I snatched that jacket and held on for dear life. Chelsea jerked me around, but I held tight. Then, as my head was being jostled all over the place, I caught a glimpse of Joe again. To my disbelief, he was loosening the straps on the light. He had no business touching that equipment. People were going to think that he was the saboteur!

I couldn't help myself. I released Chelsea's jacket and ran off the set.

"Cut!" shouted Josh. "Where's my zombie going?"

This made Joe look up. He saw me closing in and took off. Why was he running from me? I may have looked like a scary zombie, but Joe knew who I was.

I poured on the speed as Joe pulled away. He darted into another alley to try to lose me. I kept up and followed him down a short passageway, which dumped onto a busy street downtown. At the very end, he turned left.

"Ahhhhhhhh!" screamed a blond girl with earsplitting intensity.

I skidded to a stop as the sidewalk's pedestrians turned to gawk at me. Some screamed, some backed away, and some moved closer. I guess they were shocked to see a zombie in broad daylight in the middle of downtown nowhere near Halloween.

"Ah, excuse me," I said as I tried to politely push through the pack.

Unfortunately, it didn't work. No one was frightened anymore; instead they were opting to crowd around for a closer look.

"Can you take a picture with me?" asked a female voice. I glanced down to see it was the same girl who had screamed at first. Now she smiled and held up her phone.

"Maybe thome other thime," I mumbled through my zombie teeth. I was getting better at speaking with the prosthetics in my mouth.

I gazed over the crowd and could see my brother getting away, running down the sidewalk. He turned down Wilson Avenue and disappeared. It was no use trying to catch him; even if I could push through the horde, he had too big a lead on me.

I spun around to get out of there and back to the set. That's when I ran straight into . . . Joe!

"Whoa! Watch where you're going, undead dude," he said. I noticed he wasn't wearing the overalls anymore.

I pulled the teeth out of my mouth. "How did you get here?"

Joe cut his eyes to the left. "Uh . . . I walked." He looked over the gathering crowd. "They said you spazzed and ran this way." He glanced back at me. "What—are you signing autographs or something?"

I grabbed Joe's arm and pulled him into the alley with me. "I was chasing you," I whispered.

"What?" he asked.

I explained how I had seen him fooling around with the huge light and had chased after him.

My brother smiled. "Ah," he said. "That's why I came looking for you. Believe it or not, that all makes perfect sense."

CASTING THE VILLAIN

VILLAIN

10

JOE

"THAT WAS VERY UNPROFESSIONAL," scolded Josh. He and Bill glared at Frank after my brother had apologized for what seemed like the millionth time.

"I know, sir. And again, I'm very sorry," said Frank. "I just thought I saw . . ." He glanced at me and then turned his attention back to the director. "I thought I saw someone messing with that big light over there."

Bill held his radio up to his mouth. "Barry, check on that 12K, will you?"

"Copy that," replied a man's voice on the tiny speaker.

Josh rubbed his eyes. "Luckily, we can use one of the earlier takes. We're setting up for the next shot now." He grimaced at Frank. "I was going to fire you, but Chelsea reminded me about how you saved her life yesterday."

Josh said "saved her life" a little too sarcastically for my taste.

"Either way, you're done for the day," Josh continued. "If you promise not to rush off again during a take, you can continue your run as a zombie later."

"I appreciate that, sir," said Frank. "Thanks."

Josh and Bill walked back to video village, and Frank glanced around the set. "I should apologize to Chelsea," he said.

"Later," I said, tugging his tattered sleeve. "You should get out of your makeup. And after that, I have something important to show you."

We made our way to the makeup trailer and stepped inside, only to be met by ourselves! Well, almost ourselves. Both Frank's and my life casts sat on the counter, staring toward the door. They were stark white and would've looked like Greek busts of us except that they were bald and their eyes were closed.

Frank jumped when he saw them. "Very funny," he muttered.

I laughed. "I'm not punking you, bro." I pointed to the life casts. "This is what I wanted to show you."

"Yeah, I saw them the first time," said Frank. He turned to Meredith. "Will you remove my makeup, please?"

"Sure will," she replied. "But first let me show you what

we found." She waved Frank closer. "Remember I told you how we made your zombie masks?"

"Yeah," replied Frank. "You sculpted the zombie faces with clay and then took molds of those, right?"

"Right," said Meredith. "But you don't see any clay on them anymore, right?"

Even through Frank's zombie mask, I could tell he seemed a bit confused. "Right . . . so . . ."

"So Nick is very good at cleaning off the life casts when we're finished." She wiped a finger over my life cast. "These are still slimy with release agent."

"That's the stuff you use to keep the silicone molds from sticking to them, right?" asked Frank.

"Give that zombie a prize!" I joked.

Frank shook his head. "So what does it mean?"

"It means that someone else took molds of these after we did our thing," explained Meredith. "*Without* the zombie sculpts."

"So, if someone came in and took molds of just our faces . . . ," Frank began.

"I see a lightbulb going on in that undead brain of yours," I said.

Meredith smiled. "Someone could have easily made Frank and Joe Hardy masks."

Frank didn't speak as he took in the revelation. He glanced at Meredith, then at me. "So . . . you're saying that someone in the makeup department is the saboteur?"

"What?" asked Meredith. "No, not my people."

I held up both hands. "I already thought of that." I turned to Meredith. "No offense." I looked back to Frank. "Everyone here is clean. In fact, the whole makeup crew was here while you were busy chasing . . . me," I explained. "Or the guy wearing the *me* mask."

"So, where does that leave us?" asked Frank.

"It could be anyone on the crew, really," explained Meredith. "You'd be surprised at how many movie people change departments. I started in props. Nick was in production, like Hugo." She shrugged. "Any member of the crew could've learned mold making at some point. And we have all the chemicals here to do it."

Frank and I looked at each other. "There are a lot of people on the crew," I said.

Just then the door opened and Hugo poked his head in. "There you are," he said. "After you get cleaned up, Mr. Kavner wants to talk to you."

"Who's that?" I asked.

"Steve Kavner is the producer," Meredith answered. "The big cheese."

"Uh-oh," I mumbled.

Meredith removed Frank's zombie face. Once he changed out of his tattered costume, Hugo led us past the long line of trailers to an abandoned office building. At least, it was abandoned before the film crew came to town. Now it served as the production headquarters for the movie. The lobby was full of people, and the walls were decorated with actor head shots, storyboards, and production schedules.

Hugo led us to one of the larger offices in the back. He rapped on the open door and showed us inside, where a man in a blue blazer sat behind a large desk.

"Have a seat, boys," he said without looking up from his computer.

Frank and I sat in the two chairs opposite the desk. Hugo backed out, closing the door behind him.

After a short time, Mr. Kavner closed his laptop and looked us over. He removed his glasses and ran a hand through his dark hair. "So, you're the Hardy brothers I've heard so much about."

"That's us," said Frank.

I laughed nervously. "I guess that depends who you heard it from."

Kavner grinned. "Chief Olaf."

"In that case, maybe it's not us," I joked.

The producer stood and walked to the front of his desk. "No, I think you're just the guys I need to see. I had a very interesting conversation with your chief of police. He'd asked if I had met a couple of movie extras named Frank and Joe Hardy. I told him that I haven't met everyone involved with my picture, certainly not the extras. And then he asked me a very strange question. Any idea what it was?"

Frank and I glanced at each other and shook our heads.

"He asked if either of these Hardy boys had offered to

solve our little movie mystery," Kavner explained. "And when I wondered why in the world you would do such a thing, he told me that you fancy yourselves fledgling detectives."

"We are exceptional detectives," I protested.

"Joe," Frank said.

"We've probably solved more cases than Olaf has in his entire career," I continued.

"Joe," Frank repeated.

"We've solved dozens of Olaf's own cases for him," I added.

I opened my mouth to continue but felt a stab of pain in my ankle. Frank had kicked me.

Frank shrugged. "We dabble," he said modestly.

"Well, maybe you can help me out," Mr. Kavner said. "I know that you've heard about some of the shenanigans that have been going on during this production. And I know that you know about them because the chief mentioned that one of you, I forget which one, was a suspect for a short time."

"I had an alibi," Frank put in.

Mr. Kavner nodded. "Quite right. Well, maybe you can do some sleuthing for me and find out who has it in for this movie."

I wanted to tell him that we'd already made some progress on the case, but something told me to hold back. Instead I said, "Uh . . . we could do that."

Kavner threw up his hands and shook his head. "This

is unofficial, understand? I can't have anyone thinking that these accidents are anything but . . . accidents."

"Yes, sir," said Frank. I could tell by his clipped tone that he was picking up the same weird vibe as I was.

Mr. Kavner crossed his arms. "You know, if I were an unscrupulous man, I would *want* this production to shut down. My investors and I have this thing so well insured that we would probably make more money if this movie *didn't* get finished." Kavner laughed. "An unscrupulous man might even pay the saboteur or saboteurs handsomely for stopping this picture."

He stared at Frank, then at me, then back at Frank. He did this for an uncomfortably long time. Neither Frank nor I said a word.

Then Kavner laughed again. "But not me. I just want to find out who's responsible so we can stop them and finish this movie." He extended a hand to Frank. "Do we have a deal?"

Frank shook his hand. "Uh . . . yes, sir. We'll let you know if we find anything."

Then I shook hands with Mr. Kavner. "You'll be the first to know."

"Good, good," said the producer. "And make it quick, would you? I've already lost a stunt team over this."

"I thought Cody Langstrom wasn't seriously hurt," said Frank.

Kavner smiled. "I didn't mean *lose*, lose them, as if they're dead and gone. I mean that they quit. And I have a couple other departments threatening to walk off this movie as well."

Frank and I left his office and walked through the production headquarters without a word between us. Once outside, however . . .

"Was that strange, or what?" Frank asked.

"Too weird," I agreed. Then I pointed to my brother. "Dude, he *so* thinks you did it. He practically bribed you to sabotage more stuff."

"Could be," admitted Frank. "Or maybe it was some sort of test."

"What? He thought we would cop to it that easily if we were the culprits?" I asked. "I think he's been watching too many of his own movies."

Frank stopped. "Either way, we're officially on the case now."

"And if you ask me," I said, "Mr. If-I-Were-an-Unscrupulous-Man just made it to the top of the suspect list."

SCREEN CREDIT 11

FRANK

"MICHAEL ELLIOTT," I SAID. "HE'S THE SOUND mixer."

Joe tapped the virtual keys on his tablet, entering the name. He searched a couple of websites that listed all the crew members from different movies and TV shows. "Nope," said Joe. "He's just done sound."

I scratched Mr. Elliott's name off the list.

It was the following day, and neither one of us had any scenes in the movie. But that didn't stop us from working. This time we played the roles we knew all too well—detectives.

We began our investigation with a visit to the production offices, where we grabbed a crew list, and then headed out to the lunch tent. We sat down and began scanning the list for anyone who had experience working in makeup effects, specifically mold making. This method wasn't foolproof, but it was sure to eliminate most crew members.

"Barry Smith," I said. "He's the gaffer."

"What's a gaffer?" Joe asked as he typed in the name.

"The person in charge of lighting," I replied.

Joe searched the Internet for Barry's past screen credits. "No on him, too. He's just worked in electric and lighting."

I scratched Mr. Smith's name from the list.

We went through the entire list and ended up with only a handful of possible suspects. There was Bob Trevino, the special effects coordinator. At first he was near the top of the list, because he had tons of credits in prop building. Meredith had told us that prop builders make molds of things all the time. Add that to the fact that Trevino was an adamant eyewitness against Frank.

"I don't know, dude," said Joe. "He seemed pretty sincere when we talked to him."

"He didn't like anyone calling him a liar," I agreed. "What about his assistant, Chuck? He had the same brown overalls as you—or *fake* you—were wearing."

"That's a good point. But I've seen tons of crew members wearing those things," Joe explained. "The painters, some of the makeup crew . . . those overalls are everywhere."

I sighed. "True."

We went back to the crew list. There was Tom Rutherford,

the prop master for the movie. We had seen him around but hadn't had a chance to speak with him yet. And of course there was the entire makeup effects team. But Joe was steadfast in his belief that they were all innocent.

"I still think Kavner is suspicious," he offered.

"Of course," I agreed. "And having us investigate is the perfect cover."

"Plus, he has a clear motive," Joe added. "I don't see a motive with any of these other people."

We were so lost in discussion that we hadn't noticed that the movie crew had broken for lunch. People were arriving with trays of food and filling the surrounding tables.

"Frank!" shouted a voice. I turned and saw Chelsea waving me over from two tables away.

Joe nudged me. "Go get her, tiger."

I brushed him away as I walked to Chelsea's table. She wore a white robe over her wardrobe and still had the fake gash on her cheek. As soon as I approached, she locked her arm through mine and pulled me to the nearest seat.

"I'm so glad I got you alone," she said.

Don't say something stupid. Don't say something stupid, I told myself.

"Oh, okay," I said. Boy, did that sound stupid.

But Chelsea didn't seem to care. "I just wanted to thank you for what you did the other day."

"You already thanked me for pulling you off that car," I said.

"Not that." She nudged me. "For ruining that scene." She glanced around and then lowered her voice. "Was that part of the plan?"

"What plan?" I asked.

"The plan to stop the movie," she whispered. "Everyone's talking about what you two guys are doing."

"We're not . . . ," I began. "I didn't . . . we don't have any kind of plan."

Chelsea didn't seem to hear. "Did my agent hire you? I was just telling him how I wished that I'd never signed on to do this stupid movie. I mean, at first I thought it would help my image, you know? Everyone still thinks I'm a kid. I thought that a horror movie would change that." She leaned toward me. "But I didn't think the movie would be this bad. I mean, I bet it goes straight to DVD, you know? I'm just so glad that you and your brother are putting a stop to it."

"Whoa, wait," I said, somewhat surprised I got a word in. "Joe and I are not trying to stop the movie. That's not us."

Chelsea didn't reply at first. She just stared at me with her mouth agape. Finally she winked at me. "Right," she said. "Whatever you say."

She went on, telling me all about her dreams, aspirations, and future career choices. She told me how she really wanted to do a period film, but definitely no Shakespeare— he was too hard to memorize. Something more like *Abraham Lincoln: Vampire Hunter*. In her words, "You know, something classic."

I finally broke away and returned to Joe's table. After I filled him in, he asked, "Man, is there anyone who *does* want this movie to be made?"

"No kidding," I agreed.

"Bro, I hate to say it," said Joe. "But motive-wise, this puts Chelsea Alexander near the top of our suspect list."

I sighed. "I know." But honestly, it wasn't such a blow. After spending a bit more time with her, I wasn't as starstruck as I used to be.

Okay, I know that the real people are different from the characters they play on TV. I get that. And I truly didn't expect Chelsea to be as smart as her Lieutenant Fraction character. But she wasn't even as nice in real life as I thought she'd be. In fact, she only seemed to be into me after she thought I was some sort of criminal who could help her. Not cool. Still, no matter how much I got to know her, the real her, I couldn't quite shake the tiny crush I'd had since age ten.

"Let's attack this from the opposite angle," I suggested. "Who really *does* want this movie to be made?"

"The guy who wrote it and is directing it, I would think," replied Joe.

"Josh Biehn," I said. "Let's go talk to him. I could use a little positive conversation about this movie for a change."

We caught Josh in his office in the production building.

"Hey, guys," he greeted. "Come in, come in. Steve told me you were on the case."

Josh seemed like a different person. Yesterday he was about to kick me off the movie. Today he was happy to see me.

"We actually have a few questions for you, if you have time," I said.

"Sure." He sat on the edge of his desk.

"Well, first of all, to be blunt," Joe started, "do you know of anyone who would want to stop this movie?"

"That's the thing," said Josh. "I can't figure it out for the life of me."

"Well, Mr. Kavner mentioned insurance money," I said.

The director laughed. "Steve's always kidding around. And yes, this picture is well insured. But all movies are insured. And besides, there's no way he'd ruin my first picture. We go way back to when I was a stunt performer in his early films."

"Speaking of stunts, is it true that the entire stunt department has quit?" I asked.

Josh nodded and sighed. "Yeah. I can't believe Cody would run out on me like that, but he did. We go all the way back to college." He held up his hands. "But I don't blame him. He has his reputation to think of, and if someone did get hurt during one of his stunts, sabotage or not, it would be on him."

"Do you have more stunt people coming in?" I asked.

"No, there's not enough time," Josh replied. "We had to cut out most of the big stunts, and the few that are left I'll do myself."

"Isn't that kind of risky?" asked Joe. "If someone has it out for you in particular, one of your upcoming stunts would be the perfect time to strike."

"Stunts are risky, period," Josh explained. "But with you guys helping us keep an eye out, I'm sure things will go fine."

"When are the stunts happening?" I asked.

"And what are they?" asked Joe.

"Just check the call sheets," said the director. "They list all the scene numbers for the day. You can use those numbers to look them up in the script."

"Uh, we never got a script," said Joe.

Josh's eyes widened. "You didn't?" He ran to the back of his desk. "Let me get you one." He pulled open a drawer and rummaged through, pulling out a stack of pages held together with two brads. He presented it like a proud parent. "Let me know what you think."

BURNED 12

JOE

IDON'T UNDERSTAND WHY CHELSEA DOESN'T like the script," said Frank. "I mean, at the end—"

"Dude, I'm literally two pages away from the end!" I cut him off, waving the script in front of me. "Don't blow it for me."

Frank raised his hands and clamped his lips shut. He was already done up in full zombie makeup. It was weird how I was getting used to seeing him like that all the time.

Josh had only given us one copy of the script. Frank had read it the night before. Today was my turn, but I'm not as fast a reader as my brother. Now I was trying to cram in the last few pages while Nick applied my stringy zombie wig.

Finally I finished the script and put it down. "So Chelsea's character was a zombie the entire time?" I asked. "That doesn't make any sense."

Frank shook his head. "No, it's more like she's a zombie carrier."

"Or patient zero," Nick explained. "The first person to be infected."

I shrugged. "Okay, I guess that kind of makes sense."

"The point is, it's a pretty good story," said Frank. "I don't know why anyone wouldn't want it to be made."

"Yeah, I don't know either," I said. "I'd go see this movie even if I wasn't in it." When Nick moved away to get more supplies, I leaned over to Frank. "So, now that we know the whole story, where will the saboteur strike next?" I whispered.

"How about the scene we're in tonight?" Frank asked. "Isn't some old shack supposed to blow up?"

"Oh yeah," I said. "There are zombies all around, and the survivors are trying to wipe them out with an explosion." I smiled. "That'll be cool to see."

"Well, we're going to have front-row seats," said Frank.

I nodded. "Close enough to catch anyone who wants to throw a monkey wrench into the scene."

Meredith's makeup team had their work cut out for them. They had to create close to thirty zombies by nightfall, when the scene would be shot. Luckily, most of the extras didn't have as detailed masks as Frank and me. Since they wouldn't be seen up close, those extras simply wore full-face masks like you'd buy for Halloween. Our classmates—Eric,

Amanda, and Hector—were even pulled in to fill out the undead troupe.

Once the rest of the extras were ready, Hugo led us to the set. Tonight they were shooting in the vacant lot behind the Meet Locker. But the lot wasn't vacant anymore. Other than the usual lights, cameras, and crew members milling about, the lot now had a chain-link fence installed on one side. An old shack stood near the back of the lot. The run-down house looked tiny, as if it had only a couple of rooms. It also looked as if it had been standing there for fifty years or more. But since I had grown up in Bayport, I knew for a fact that it hadn't been there a week ago.

Hugo led us to the chain-link fence while the camera crew gathered on the other side.

"Okay, zombies!" Bill shouted. "In this scene, we're going to have you trying to get through the fence and away from the shack. The shack is going to catch fire, burn for a bit, and then explode."

I glanced back at the shack. It was at the other end of the lot, about forty yards away. Several of the other zombie extras were looking back as well.

Bill answered the question that I'm sure was on many of our minds. "Don't worry, you'll be fine." He gestured to Bob Trevino. "And with that, I'm going to turn it over to Bob for the safety speech."

The special effects coordinator stepped up. "I've done these gags a hundred times, and they're perfectly safe. The building is mostly made of lightweight balsa wood, and the charges we've placed are very controlled. You're about triple the distance past the debris field."

Frank raised a hand, and Bill nodded to him. Luckily, by now we had learned to leave out our prosthetic teeth until right before shooting began. "Won't it look like we're too far away?" my brother asked.

"That's why we're shooting this scene with a long lens," Bill replied. "Whenever you see actors running from an explosion, it's mostly shot with a telephoto lens. The optics compress the scene so it looks like the background is right on top of the foreground."

I smiled at Frank. "Cool."

He glanced around. "Let's just keep an eye out for anything out of the ordinary," he whispered.

"Yeah," I murmured. "And what's more ordinary than a bunch of zombies and an exploding building?"

"We're only going to get one shot at this, people," Bill went on. "So we're going to rehearse the cues." He went on to explain just what he wanted us to do. When he was finished, Josh stepped forward.

"Okay, let's try one," said Josh.

"Rehearsal's up!" shouted Bill.

Josh returned to his chair behind the monitors. "And . . . action!"

All of us zombies clawed at the fence, moaning and pushing ourselves up against the metal links.

"Okay, cue the fire!" Josh shouted.

"The fire ignites," barked Bob. He stood by the director and held a small box with wires snaking out of the top. The thin brown wires led to the ground, around the fence, and to the shack.

As instructed, none of us zombies noticed when the fire ignited. We continued to paw at the fence.

"It's going to burn for a while," said Josh. "A little more . . . and . . . cue the explosion!"

"Boom!" shouted Bob.

Even though this was just a rehearsal, we zombies flung ourselves at the fence as if we were hit from behind. Then we collapsed in a heap, truly lifeless.

"And cut!" shouted Josh. He sprung from his chair. "Let's get ready to go for real."

"Meredith," said Bill. "You want to check your makeup before we go?"

"Copy that," replied Meredith. She and her team swooped toward the zombies.

We all laughed as we climbed off one another. I stood and extended a hand to Frank. "I didn't hurt you too much, did I?"

Frank groaned as he climbed to his feet. "No, but I think you should lay off the craft service for the rest of the movie."

I didn't really register what Frank had said because I was too busy staring at something bizarre. I tapped him on the shoulder and pointed to the shack. "Check it out," I whispered.

Two figures in brown overalls slunk across the lot toward the shack. But what made the scene truly weird was the fact that the two figures were *us*.

We watched ourselves open the front door, look around, and duck inside.

"Let's go," hissed Frank. He darted toward the old building.

I stayed with him as we sprinted across the lot. When he reached the front door, he carefully opened it and ducked inside. I followed him in and quietly closed the door behind me. I didn't want the saboteurs to know we were in the shack with them.

Of course, after we were actually inside, I could see that it would have been impossible to remain hidden from anyone already in there. From the outside, the old house looked like it had a few rooms. But since this was a movie set and only the outside mattered, it was essentially just one big room. The wood inside looked new, and several long boards propped up the walls around us. There wasn't even a floor; bare dirt was beneath our feet. We were also completely alone.

"Where did they go?" I asked.

"There!" Frank pointed to a door at the other end of the open room. We hopped over several large pipes as we crossed the space. I beat Frank to the door and grabbed the knob. It wouldn't budge.

We looked all around the open structure. Support boards crisscrossed everywhere, but there was no place for one person to hide, let alone two.

My eyes fell on the large pipes littering the floor. They were capped but had huge holes drilled into the sides. Thin brown wires snaked out of the caps and wound their way through small holes in the walls. Other wires connected to bags of liquid taped under the front windows. I recognized those wires right away and realized where they led: right to the small controller box in Bob Trevino's hands.

My stomach dropped to around my knees as I realized that this place was rigged to blow.

Outside, a distant voice shouted, "Okay, here we go!" It was Bill Daines.

Frank's eyes widened. We ran back to the front door. This time Frank got there first. He grasped the knob and turned. Nothing happened. He pulled and jerked the doorknob frantically. Nothing.

We were trapped inside.

Back with the crew, another shout. "And . . . action!"

THE BIG SCORE

13

FRANK

POUNDED ON THE FRONT DOOR. "HEY!" I SHOUTED. "We're in here!"

"They're not going to hear you over the zombie groans," said Joe. "Remember how loud it was out there?"

He was right. We were far away from the zombie horde outside—triple the distance past the debris field, from what Bob Trevino had said. A safe distance away.

That is, *they* were a safe distance away. Joe and I were at ground zero.

"Try the other door again," I ordered.

Joe ran across the open house and jerked at the back door. He even kicked it a few times. "It's not moving," he reported. He ran back to me and pointed at one of the windows in the front. "Let's try the window."

"Good idea," I said. After all, if we couldn't open it, at least we could break through.

As we moved toward the window, we heard Bill shout again. "Okay, Bob. Cue the fire."

There was a loud pop near the window, and then flames erupted under the sill. They raced up both sides, blocking our escape. Another pop and the second window was engulfed in more flames. Joe and I moved to the center of the structure as fire burst around us.

"We have to get out of here, bro!" cried Joe. "This thing is going to blow."

"Ram the door, on three," I said. "One, two, three!"

We slammed into the door. Pain erupted in my shoulder, but the door barely budged.

"What else you got?" sputtered Joe, coughing as smoke filled the room.

Both of us backed away from the burning walls. The heat was unbearable. I glanced around, looking for any way out. Then I spotted two white buckets near a wall that wasn't covered with flames. I ran to them and threw off one of the lids. The bucket was full of a clear substance. I thrust my hand inside and felt a thick gel.

"Come here!" I ordered as I picked up the bucket. When Joe was near, I dumped the contents over his head.

"Stunt gel!" exclaimed Joe.

I pointed to the other bucket. "Now, do me."

Joe grabbed the other bucket, ripped off the lid, and

poured its contents over my head. Immediately, everything felt cooler.

"This helps, but I don't think it's going to protect us from the explosion," I said.

Joe pointed to one of the walls. "Look!"

The smoke was thick, but I could just make out the crisscross pattern on one wall. Flames licked up the sides, but it didn't burn. It was Sheetrock. And the pattern was similar to the ones Bob Trevino's assistant had been making with the circular saw.

"That's our shot," I said. "On three . . ."

"On one!" Joe corrected. "One!"

We ran full speed for the wall. I fought every instinct to slow down as we neared it. We had to trust that the wall was scored for a reason. We hit the wall hard but didn't stop, bursting through the Sheetrock and into the cool air outside. Joe and I tumbled to the ground. I scrambled to my feet and pulled him up behind me. We ran ten more feet, then . . .

KA-BOOM!

Light bloomed around us as we were shoved forward by the blast. We hit the ground hard and tumbled as bits of splintered wood rained down on us. Luckily, Bob had been right; the light balsa debris didn't hurt at all.

"And cut!" Josh shouted.

At the other end of the lot, the movie crew erupted in applause. Meanwhile, Joe and I caught our breath and staggered to our feet.

"We almost get killed and they applaud?" Joe asked.

I would've replied, but I was still out of breath.

Bill, Josh, and several other crew members crossed the lot.

"That looked amazing!" Josh shouted. He turned to Bill. "You didn't tell me we had our stunt performers back."

Bill frowned. "We didn't. These are the Hardys."

Bob ran up to us. "What were you doing in there?" he asked. "That set was supposed to be cleared."

I explained what had happened.

"There was supposed to be a stunt just like what you did," explained Bob. "A couple of zombies were going to be stuck in the shack. We had the set prepped for that days ago, before the stunt team walked off the picture."

I rubbed a bruised arm. "I'm glad you did. Otherwise, we'd still be in there." I turned to look at the burning pile of lumber that had been the old shack.

SHOOTING SCRIPT 14

JOE

A HUGE PLATE OF BACON APPEARED before me. But this wasn't any ordinary plate of bacon. The strips had been arranged to form two stars.

"Thanks, Aunt T," I said.

"Yeah, this is great," added Frank.

"A special breakfast for our two movie stars," clucked Aunt Trudy.

"We're not stars, Aunt Trudy," Frank corrected. "We're just a couple of zombie extras. Two of many."

"Well, it's nice to have at least one morning where we can all eat breakfast together," said Mom. "I didn't think we'd get any time with you over this spring break, with your movie work and all."

"In a couple of days it'll be back to school, with just a banana on the go for breakfast," Aunt Trudy added, shaking her head.

"It says here there was a big explosion on the set last night," announced our dad from the other side of a newspaper.

Frank and I glanced at each other. We had made a pact not to tell our parents about our close call the night before. We certainly didn't want them to worry.

"It was all part of the movie," Frank explained. "They built this old house just to blow it up for a stunt."

"Well, even though it's not exactly my kind of movie, I can't wait to see you boys on the big screen," said Mom with a smile.

"You won't be able to recognize us when you do," Frank said. "We're both in zombie makeup for most of it."

"Yeah, walking corpses," I added. "Decomposing flesh . . . that sort of thing."

Mom shivered. "Not at the table, dear."

Our dad folded the paper and placed it by his plate. "You know, since that movie came to town, the *Bayport Bugle* has become a regular gossip column."

"They're just trying to drum up business," said Aunt Trudy, passing around a plate of scrambled eggs.

"Still," Dad continued, "there's talk of all kinds of mayhem over there."

I could feel Frank's gaze on me but made sure I didn't glance at him. "Oh yeah?" I asked between bites of eggs.

wanted to mess with the wiring. Keep it from blowing up. Or have it blow up where someone might've been hurt."

Frank seemed to think about this for a while. "They could've seen us coming through the windows. Maybe they ducked out the back and didn't get a chance to destroy anything."

"It makes sense," I agreed. "And who would know what to mess up better than a special effects guy?"

"Bob Trevino," said Frank.

"He might know something. I'll talk to him while you talk to Chelsea," I offered.

"Sounds like a plan." Frank nodded.

Once we arrived, my brother took off to find Chelsea while I headed to the special effects trailer.

I found Bob and his crew cleaning equipment in the back of their trailer. The look on Bob's face when he saw me reinforced my belief that he wasn't our guy. He wore an expression of concern mixed with a hint of shame.

"Hey, Joe," he greeted me, stepping forward to shake my hand. "How are you guys doing? And look, seems I owe you an apology. I could have sworn it was Frank I saw sneaking around behind that building set, but the police say his alibi checks out."

"We're fine," I replied. "And apology accepted. Right now we're trying to figure out who *is* responsible for the sabotage. I just wanted to ask you a few questions about the explosion."

Our dad was a retired private investigator, after all. There wasn't much he missed.

"Probably a publicity stunt," Aunt Trudy added.

"I'm surprised you haven't heard gossip about Chelsea Alexander dating a local guy," I said, changing the subject. Frank's eyes widened. I shrugged and gave him a look as if to say, *Sorry, bro, you need to take one for the team right now.*

"Oh, really?" asked Mom. She looked at Frank and smiled. I guess she remembered my brother's massive childhood crush too. "Anyone we know?"

Frank shook his head. "Don't look at me."

A small beep chirped from his pocket. He pulled out his phone and read a text. His thumbs flew over the screen as he replied.

"Not at the table," scolded Aunt Trudy.

"Sorry, Aunt Trudy," he apologized, typing a few more characters and then putting the phone away. "It's about the movie." He stood and downed the rest of his juice before taking his plate to the sink. "We have to go."

"What's up?" I asked.

Frank looked back at the table nervously. All eyes were on him. "I have to help someone run lines."

"Run lines? What does that mean?" asked our aunt.

"That's movie talk for actors practicing their dialogue," I explained.

"Oh?" Mom smiled at me, then up at Frank. "Run lines with whom?"

Frank's shoulders dropped, and he stared at the floor. "Chelsea Alexander."

I cleared my plate as Frank was subjected to all kinds of questions from Mom and Aunt Trudy. You'd think that he was the star and they were paparazzi. They wanted to know all about his brush with stardom—and about Chelsea Alexander in particular. Once he'd fielded their questions with a lot of "I don't knows" and "I'll have to asks," we gathered our things and headed outside.

As Frank led the way to his car, he shook his head. "Why did you have to tell them about Chelsea?"

"Dude, you know why," I replied. "Dad was about to ask if we were working this case."

Frank sighed. "Yeah, I know."

"Either way, you know we can't lie to Dad," I said. Not only was lying to our parents something we didn't want to do, but our dad had logged countless hours in the interrogation room. He would've seen right through any story we could have come up with. It was best to avoid the line of questioning entirely.

Just as we were almost to the car, we heard a voice behind us. "Boys," our dad called from the front stoop.

"Yeah, Dad?" I asked.

He took a sip from his coffee cup. "Good luck today," he said. "And be careful."

"Okay, thanks," called Frank as he climbed behind the wheel.

"Bye!" I waved.

Once both doors were shut, we looked at e smiled.

"He totally knows," I said.

Frank started the car. "Can't get anything Hardy."

As we drove across town toward the set what's the game plan?"

"I'm going to help Chelsea run lines," Fra

I raised an eyebrow. "And . . ."

"And see what she knows about wha night," Frank added. "After all, she wasn't on set yesterday. I want to find out where s

"You don't think she was one of the sal I asked.

"I don't think so," he replied. "The fak were too tall. But she still might know som her agent told her something."

Frank had told me how Chelsea th might've hired us to sabotage the proc know we're not the culprits, maybe her a someone.

"I've been thinking a lot about last nig it wasn't a trap after all."

"It sure felt like one," said Frank.

"No kidding. But what if the two . . just planning to wreck the place?" I sug

The night before, Frank and I had explained that we'd seen two figures enter the building. We didn't tell them about the masks they wore; we didn't want anyone to think we were nuts, after all.

Trevino rubbed the back of his neck. "I still feel terrible about that. Safety is my main concern. I have never had anything like that happen before. I should've been watching the building more closely."

"I understand," I said. "What I don't understand is what someone could've done to sabotage that set."

Bob thought for a moment. "Well, we ignited the flames using blasting caps and spark hits. Spark hits are tiny explosives that make a giant spark when they go off. The blasting caps blew apart plastic bags of flammable liquid and the sparks ignited them."

I smiled. "Yeah, we got a front-row seat for that." I could see guilt begin to wash over the man's face again, so I changed the subject. "So what about the explosion?"

"Those were a bunch of can poppers," he explained. "They're basically devices that pop open small propane tanks. We added some more spark hits to ignite the propane. Normally, they're very safe."

"So how could someone mess that up?" I asked.

"I suppose someone could've rewired everything to go at once," he suggested. "It wouldn't be difficult, but you'd have to know what to look for."

"Like someone in special effects?" I asked.

Bob raised an eyebrow. "Yeah, but all my guys were with me at the time, manning fire extinguishers. I was by the director, triggering the fires and explosion."

"Who else would know what to do?" I asked.

"Well, anyone who has worked in special effects before," he said.

Oh boy. That put us back to cross-checking the crew list with the Internet. I wasn't looking forward to that again.

"The stunt department would be familiar with the setup," he added. "But they pulled out days ago. And frankly, I'm thinking about doing the same. This picture has too many wild cards involved to suit me."

I thanked him and headed back to the makeup trailer to meet Frank, who would head there as soon as he could break away from Chelsea. As I walked, I mulled the clues over in my mind.

The first accident took place during a stunt. The second accident was a sabotaged set, which anyone could have figured out. But the third involved special effects. According to Bob, any stunt performer would be familiar enough with pyrotechnics to be able to rewire them. That covered the knowledge needed for two of the three accidents. The stunt team had quit, but there was still one stunt performer left on the show—or former stunt performer: the director, Josh Biehn.

Something Aunt Trudy had mentioned over breakfast stuck out in my mind. She said the accidents were probably some sort of publicity stunt. And a new director could use all the publicity he could get for his first film.

When I arrived at the trailer, I found Meredith and her team busy creating more zombie and body parts. It seemed that there was never any downtime for their department. Frank was already there.

"Any luck with Chelsea?" I asked.

"She was out shopping with her assistant all day. And still thinks her agent hired us." Frank shook his head. "She's thrilled but realizes that I can't talk about it. There were a lot of winks and the use of the phrase 'need-to-know basis.'"

I told him about what I'd learned from Bob as well as my suspicions about Josh.

"That makes a lot of sense," he admitted. "And he could've hired a couple of guys to do it. But it doesn't explain the use of the Hardy masks."

"I've been thinking about that," I said. "We've been seen around the set a lot, so the saboteurs probably used the masks so that they would blend in, right?"

"Yeah," said Frank.

"And if they ever got busted and had to get away, all they'd have to do is dump the masks and overalls," I explained. "Then they could just blend into the crew."

Frank nodded and reached into his pocket. He pulled out a call sheet. "Well, we can ask him for sure when we catch him in the act. When's the next sabotage-worthy scene?"

I looked over his shoulder and read what was scheduled

for today. It didn't give much in the way of description, but it did list the scene numbers. I opened my backpack and pulled out our copy of the movie script. I thumbed through it, looking for scene numbers. Each scene in the movie script had a header, but no numbers.

"These aren't supposed to be page numbers, are they?" I asked.

"Hey, Meredith," said Frank. "Where are the scene numbers in a script?"

Meredith came over and glanced at the script. "Oh, that must be an early script," she said. "When you write a script, you don't number the scenes. The scenes get numbered after a script goes into production. That's called a shooting script."

Frank dug into his backpack and pulled out a script. "I still have the copy Chelsea gave me to run lines with earlier."

He opened it, and sure enough, each scene had a header and a number. We compared the numbers with the shooting schedule for the day. Each scene for the day seemed pretty simple. They took place in abandoned buildings and mainly just had dialogue. No stunts or special effects.

Frank pointed to the bottom of the call sheet. "They give you a preview of tomorrow's schedule here." He pointed to a row of scene numbers and descriptions. It also listed what departments would be needed.

I scanned through the scene numbers and thumbed through the production script. I quickly found what we were looking for.

"Tomorrow they're shooting that big scene in the airplane hangar," I noted.

"Oh yeah," said Frank. "That's the one where Chelsea's character flips that armored car."

"And she survives?" I raised both hands. "Because she was a zombie the entire time."

"See, I told you it made sense," Frank said. "Either way, that stunt is first up in the morning."

I scanned the call sheet. "It says here that Josh will be the stunt driver." I looked up and shook my head. "How could he play Chelsea's character?"

"I can show you," said Meredith.

She opened a cabinet and carefully pulled out a Chelsea mask. Just like the Frank and Joe masks, it had a full head of hair and everything. I have to admit, it was cool but kind of creepy.

Frank and I looked at each other. "So, stunt performers wear these kinds of masks?"

"All the time," said Meredith. "In fact, Josh was very interested when we made this particular mask. He seemed to know the process, even." She shook her head and left the room.

"Well, if they shoot that stunt first thing in the morning," I whispered, "if I were a saboteur, I'd go out there tonight."

I shoved the shooting script into my backpack just as Meredith returned. "You really should have Josh sign that early script," she suggested, pointing to the script still in my hand. "If this movie actually gets finished, it could be a collector's item."

I smiled at Frank. "Wouldn't be a bad idea," I whispered, pointing to the director's name on the cover page. "Think of how much more it'll be worth if he's arrested for sabotaging his own movie."

Frank looked at the cover page, and his eyes widened. "I don't think he's going to be arrested," he said. "Because he's not our guy. Look."

He pointed to the cover page. When I saw what was written on it, my eyes widened.

"So how do you want to play this?" I asked Frank.

Frank smiled. "I think I have an idea," he replied. "It's going to take careful planning, impeccable timing, and a few special effects of our own."

"Copy that," I said.

"Meredith, can you make up a few Frank and Joe Hardy masks for us?" Frank asked.

Meredith smiled. "Sure. If you'll help."

"Deal." Frank pointed to me. "Call Eric, Hector, and Amanda. See if they want to play a part in *our* production."

FRANK

KAY, THIS IS REALLY FREAKY," JOE
said with a muffled voice.

"You're telling me," I replied.

At that moment, looking at my brother
was one of the most surreal moments of my
life. It was as if I was looking into a mirror, or at least a
carnival mirror. Joe wore a Frank Hardy mask. The face was
expressionless and seemed a little fake, of course, but every
detail was perfect, right down to the chicken pox scar by my
hairline. It was so detailed because it was pulled from a mold
made of my life cast this afternoon. I knew Joe probably felt
the same way, because I was wearing a Joe Hardy mask. We
looked at each other, at ourselves, both dressed in identical
brown overalls, also on loan from the makeup department.

"If I were in therapy, this would be worth two, maybe three entire sessions," said Joe.

We crouched behind a large cart loaded with light stands and gazed at the dark airplane hangar. Apparently, the Bayport Airport had rented out the unused hangar to the production company. There were no planes, but the hanger was full of equipment, sets, and props for tomorrow's shoot. Two vehicles were parked in the center of the large structure: a beat-up pickup truck and an armored car. Both would be featured in scenes bright and early tomorrow morning. If the movie's saboteurs were going to hit something, it would be one or both of those vehicles. Mr. Kavner had given us keys to the hangar so we could stake it out and wait for the culprits.

Joe and I waited an hour or so before trying on the masks. Since they'd been created that day, Meredith had instructed us to wait until the last moment. It's good that we hadn't had them on the entire time, because they were hot, hard to breathe through, and even harder to see through.

Luckily, I could still make out all the hangar's exits. There was the giant main door, big enough for planes to pull through, which we had locked down first thing. And there were also four small side doors. A set of metal stairs led up the back wall to a suspended office with large glass windows.

We didn't have to wait long. Shortly after nightfall, a side door opened and . . . *we* walked through. The other Frank and Joe walked to the center of the hangar, split up, and headed for both vehicles.

"Everything else in place?" I asked.

Although I saw my own face staring blankly back at me, I could hear a smile in Joe's voice. "Oh yeah."

"Go for it," I instructed.

Joe kept low as he jogged toward the side door, the same one that the other Frank and Joe had just entered through. Next to the door was a large metal breaker box. Once he had covered the distance, he grabbed the handle on the side of the box and pushed it up.

CLACK!

The hangar's lights blazed to life.

"Okay, you two," Joe yelled. "Give it up. The real Hardy boys have you surrounded!"

The two crooks scrambled out from under the cars and started toward the door from which they'd entered. They spotted Joe (or me) blocking the exit, then split up. The one dressed as Joe darted for the door on the next wall. It looked like an easy escape.

When he was a few yards away, the door swung open and Joe stepped into the light. At least, it looked like Joe. It was really our friend Amanda wearing a Joe mask and overalls. The crook skidded to a stop, turned, and sprinted across the hangar for the opposite door.

Meanwhile, the taller crook, the one wearing my face,

dashed for the next closest door. Before he was twenty yards away, it opened and "I" stepped into the light. But it was really Hector wearing a Frank Hardy mask. The crook slid to a stop and began backing away.

That was my cue. I sprang from my hiding place and ran toward the crook in my mask. When I was close, I veered away and jogged toward the metal stairs on the back wall.

"This way!" I said, and beckoned for him to follow.

I didn't have to look back to know that our plan was working. I could hear the saboteur's footsteps close behind. Since I wore my brother's mask and the crook wore my mask, Joe and I had hoped that the saboteur would think that I was his partner in crime. This way, I could lure him away from the others. I clanked up the metal steps two at a time. By now, the other crook would have found the final exit blocked by Eric, wearing my mask. The Hardy boys really did have him surrounded.

I reached the landing and threw open the office door. The abandoned room was littered with broken office furniture and scraps of paper. Dim fluorescent bulbs flickered above, casting the scene in fractured light. Brighter light streamed through the large plate-glass windows overlooking the hangar.

The crook's footsteps were close, so I stepped aside behind the open door. Once the figure tore through the doorway, I slammed the door shut and locked the dead bolt.

The other me glanced around the room. "Where to now?" he demanded in a muffled voice.

"How about jail?" I asked as I removed my Joe mask.

Police sirens wailed in the distance, making the criminal search the room frantically for an escape route. I knew there wasn't one. Joe and I had scouted out the entire hangar beforehand. Everything was going perfectly according to plan.

The other me picked up a broken chair and raised it over his head. He stepped forward. I raised my arms, bracing for the attack. But instead of striking me, the crook threw the chair at the window.

CRASH!

The glass shattered and he dove out of the office.

"This wasn't part of the plan," I muttered as I ran toward the window.

I expected to see the figure fall to the hangar floor below, but instead he shuffled across a thin metal catwalk. It was made of wire mesh and extended all the way across the hangar. The catwalk was suspended by rows of thin cables and ended just under a bunch of small windows. So there was an escape route after all.

"This is crazy," I mumbled as I shimmied out after him.

The catwalk was so narrow that the crook couldn't run,

but he had a good lead on me. I reached out and grabbed the thin cables as I moved farther and farther out over the open hangar. Every step seemed to make the thing wobble.

When the other me was halfway across the hangar, he turned back. "Leave me alone," he growled. Then he grabbed two cables and swung his hips.

The catwalk swayed beneath me. My right foot slipped, and I gasped as I struggled to hold on to one of the cables. The hangar below blurred as my foot dangled into space. I tightened my lips and pulled myself back up. Once both feet were planted, I continued to move toward the saboteur.

The crook didn't budge. Instead he stared at me as if he couldn't believe I was still following him. The police sirens were deafening as red and blue lights streaked across the hangar windows.

"It's too late," I said, staring myself in the face. I inched closer. "The cops are here now. There's nowhere to run."

The other me let me take a few steps closer before he shook the catwalk again. This time I was ready for him. I held tightly to two cables. Seeing that I couldn't be shaken free, he jumped up and down.

"I've fallen from higher places than this," said the other me. "How about you?"

PANG!

A support cable snapped.

PANG-PANG!

Then two more. I leaned back as one whipped past my face. This time both feet came off the catwalk as it tipped to the side. My hands ached as I held tight to the cables.

CRACK!

The catwalk snapped and fell away.

FACE-OFF 16

JOE

THE OTHER ME WAS CORNERED. NO MATTER where he ran, the exits were covered by a Frank, a Joe, and another Frank. Each of us moved closer and closer, boxing him in toward the center of the airplane hangar. It must have really freaked him out, because the fake me finally backed against the armored car and slumped to the ground. The police sirens grew louder. He knew he was whipped.

"You think this is weird," I said, stepping closer to the crook. "Check this out." I removed my mask, revealing my own face. I pointed to Hector (wearing a Joe mask). "See? Just like that handsome devil over there."

CRASH!

A chair burst through one of the plate-glass windows

above. The chair and bits of glass clattered to the floor. Then I saw Frank jump through the window and onto a thin catwalk.

"Frank?!" I cried.

Another Frank followed him out. They were so high that I couldn't make out which was the real Frank and which was the fake. The two shimmied across the thin walkway.

With our attention diverted, the fake me scrambled to his feet and took off running. I tore after him as he headed for the nearest exit. Luckily, the airplane hangar was huge, so he wasn't getting away that easily. Add that to the fact that I'm a decent runner and I was able to slowly close the gap between us. Then, just when we were ten feet from the door, I leaped forward. I tackled him around the waist and we flew through the open doorway. We tumbled across the asphalt, coming to a stop in the beams of police car head-lights. The perp moaned as he lay crumpled on the ground. Pain blasted from my right knee as I slowly got to my feet.

"Frank!" came Eric's voice from inside.

I left the crumpled crook on the ground and limped back to the hangar door. I felt like I had been punched in the gut when I took in the scene above me. Cables snapped off the catwalk, and the thin walkway began to bow. Both Franks held on for dear life.

I half ran, half limped toward them, but it was too late. Amanda screamed as Frank lost his grip and fell away from the catwalk.

"Frank!" I screamed. I forgot the pain in my knee and sprinted faster.

Frank's arms and legs flailed as he dropped from above. His body slammed into the top of the armored truck with enough force to make the heavy vehicle jostle on its shocks. His body lay on the roof with one arm dangling over the side.

"Frank!" I shouted as I ran up to the truck. I climbed onto the running board and grabbed the roof. I pulled my head up to see my brother's face staring back at me. Only it wasn't really my brother's face.

It was just a mask.

"Hey," said a voice from above.

My head snapped up and I saw Frank—the real Frank—holding tightly to what was left of the catwalk.

"A little help here?" he said with a weak smile.

Hector and Eric ran toward the stairs just as Bayport's finest filed into the hangar. I watched as our friends helped Frank climb back through the office window. When the three marched down the steps, I heard a familiar voice behind me.

"How did I guess that an anonymous tip would lead me right to Frank and Joe Hardy?" asked Chief Olaf.

I shrugged. "You're just that good of a detective, Chief."

"Right." The chief eyed me suspiciously. "Okay, boys." He looked around the hangar. "You care to tell me just what went on here tonight?"

Frank and I explained how we had staked out the hangar, figuring it was the most logical place for the saboteurs to strike next. We then explained how the crooks used masks pulled from our life casts to hide their identities during the crimes.

"You can ask makeup artist Meredith Banks," I said. "She'll tell you how they did it."

"That's why Trevino identified you," the chief said to Frank. Then he pointed to the mask in Amanda's hand. "And you had these masks made up . . . why?"

"To fight fire with fire," Frank explained.

"Plus, it totally confused them," I added. "They didn't know which of us was their partner in crime."

While we were speaking, an ambulance arrived and paramedics pushed a ladder against the top of the armored truck. One of them used scissors to carefully cut away the Frank mask. The face underneath belonged to Cody Langstrom, the movie's former stunt coordinator, now unconscious.

Frank went on to explain how he'd led Cody upstairs to confront him. Cody had fled onto the catwalk, and when Frank had followed, the stuntman tried to knock him off. Eric, Amanda, and Hector had seen the entire thing.

"The guy outside is Chase Wilkes," said Olaf. "Do you know him?"

"We met him once," I said. "He was one of the stunt performers."

"So why did these guys want to sabotage the movie?" asked Eric.

"We have our suspicions," replied Frank. "But you'll have to ask Josh Biehn to be sure."

Hector glanced at his watch. "Who should be here any minute. When the crooks arrived, I sent Hugo a text to get him here ASAP."

Before the director arrived, the paramedics looked us over. Frank had some friction burns on his palms from the cables. I just had some scrapes and bruises from my chase with Chase. I was icing my knee with a cold pack when Josh and Mr. Kavner entered the hangar.

"What's going on here?" asked Mr. Kavner. "Josh got a text saying our set was being destroyed."

I looked at Frank and cringed. "I didn't think Hugo would say that," I whispered.

"The Hardys unmasked the culprits, as it were," Chief Olaf said, and glanced at his notepad. "Chase Wilkes and Cody Langstrom."

"Cody?" asked Josh.

Olaf gestured to us. "The boys think you would know why he did it."

Josh looked at us and nodded.

"We saw his name on the early script's title page," Frank offered. "He co-wrote the movie with you, didn't he?"

The director sucked in a breath. "Yes. Well, the original script. A long time ago." He rubbed the back of his neck. "We thought up the story more than ten years ago. We worked on it a little, but Cody lost interest along the way, while I kept at it, doing rewrite after rewrite. I finally secured the funding, set everything up. I made it happen. But by that time it was a different movie entirely. Cody still wanted credit, even after I did all the work. I guess I thought I'd made him happy by appointing him the stunt coordinator, but I was wrong."

Chief Olaf cut us loose while he took statements from Josh and Mr. Kavner. Everyone was kind enough to keep my slow pace as I limped out to Frank's car. Once there, Frank turned to the others and held out his hand.

"Okay, you guys," he muttered. "Hand them over."

Amanda grinned. "Hand what over?"

"You know what," I said. "The masks. This town is only big enough for two Hardy brothers."

Hector shook his head. "No way, man. This is gonna be my Halloween costume this year." He put on his Frank mask.

"Hey," said Frank.

Eric put on his Frank mask. "This is my new Facebook profile pic, yo."

"Great idea," said Amanda. She put on her Joe mask and placed her hands on her hips. "Besides, I think this is a good look for me."

I held up a hand, blocking my view of her. "Okay, now you're just creeping me out."

"Yeah," Frank agreed. "My brother's head on a girl's body is just wrong."

She waved and backed away. Hector and Eric turned and followed.

"Let's go solve a mystery, guys," Hector yelled.

We watched them (us) climb into Eric's truck and pull away. Amanda hung out the window, blowing us kisses while wearing the *me* mask.

"Okay, I'm going to have nightmares about that," said Frank. "Seriously."

I opened the passenger door and climbed in. "Dude, I hate to see what we get blamed for next."

OPENING NIGHT

17

FRANK

I ANGLED THE REARVIEW MIRROR TO MAKE SURE MY tie was straight.

"Hey," said Joe as he adjusted his own tie. "I was using that."

"My car," I said. "I go first."

Normally, I wouldn't have been so short, but let's face it, I was nervous. It had been six months since the movie had wrapped, and tonight was its big premiere. Despite all the difficulties, Josh Biehn had decided to have its first showing right here in Bayport. A bunch of crew members were going to be there, and any Bayport citizen who had taken part had received a special invitation to the premiere. Of course, I wasn't nervous to see myself on the silver screen; I was nervous because Chelsea Alexander was going to be there.

Yes, I know. Chelsea didn't turn out to be as perfect in real life as I had hoped she'd be. She had her faults. But hey, who didn't? Besides, how often does anyone get to be friends with a beautiful movie star? Okay, I'll admit it. I still hadn't totally outgrown my ten-year-old crush.

I straightened my tie and spun the mirror back to face Joe.

"Relax, man," said Joe. "Play it cool."

"I am playing it cool," I said.

Joe pointed behind him. "You think that's playing it cool?"

I glanced back at the small bouquet of flowers lying on the backseat. "It's just being polite," I claimed. "Welcoming her back to our town."

Joe stared at me with his patented *you're going with that?* look.

I climbed out of the car and opened the back door. I put on my suit coat and grabbed the bouquet. Joe fell into step beside me as we walked across the parking lot.

The theater's lobby was crowded with smartly dressed people. It was great seeing several of the crew members again. We caught up with Meredith and Nick and even said hello to Bob Trevino. All our fellow extras were there, including Amanda, Eric, and Hector.

"I almost wore the mask," Hector whispered.

"You still have that thing?" I asked.

"I'm saving it for a special occasion," he replied.

"Are those for me?" Amanda asked, pointing to the flowers.

I put them behind my back. "Uh . . ."

Joe grinned. "You know who they're for."

Eric looked around. "Chelsea's here? I haven't seen her yet."

"Me neither," I agreed. I had been scanning the crowd ever since we got there but hadn't spotted her. I wanted to give her the flowers discreetly, so I kept close watch on the doors.

When it was time for the movie to begin, I hung back while everyone made his or her way to the main theater. Finally, when I was the last one in the lobby, I gave up and headed into the theater.

The place was packed, but Joe had saved me a seat among our other friends. I craned my neck to look around, but I still didn't see Chelsea. Then the audience applauded, and I turned my attention to the screen. Josh Biehn stood in front of it, waving.

When the applause died, Josh gave a small bow and said, "Thank you. And thank you all for coming. As with any motion picture, there were certain challenges to getting this made. Sometimes location can be the biggest challenge of all, but Bayport welcomed us from the beginning, and we cherished every part of our time here. Even if we did have to destroy some of it to make this movie."

Everyone laughed.

"But seriously," he continued. "I want to give a special thanks to two people who helped us overcome a particular challenge. And I daresay that without their help, I couldn't have finished this movie. A big thanks to Joe and Frank Hardy."

The audience applauded around us. It was a little embarrassing. Well, for me at least. Joe waved to everyone, soaking up all the attention.

Once the applause died down again, Josh continued, "Now, before we watch the film"—he gave a sly grin—"I want to read an e-mail I received on your behalf from the star, Chelsea Alexander." He reached into his coat and pulled out a folded piece of paper.

I have to admit that even though I was disappointed, part of me was a little relieved. Now I didn't have to worry about how she'd react to the stupid flowers I'd been carrying around all night.

Josh cleared his throat. "Dear Bayport, I'm sorry I couldn't be there on your special night, but I'm in the middle of shooting my next movie and just couldn't break away. I want to thank you for your hospitality. But I want to give a special thanks to one of you in particular: my rehearsal partner and my personal zombie bodyguard . . . Fred Hardy."

Fred? *Fred* Hardy? Even though the audience applauded politely, I sank into my chair with embarrassment.

"Oh, man," whispered Joe. "That burns. Sorry, bro."

Hector reached over and shook my shoulder. "Dude, I know what I'm going to do with my mask," he said. "I'm going to mail it to Chelsea, so she'll always remember what *Fred* Hardy looks like."

I nodded. "Good one."

Josh clasped his hands together. "All right then. On with the show!" He took his seat and the lights dimmed.

As the opening credits rolled, I glanced down at the stupid bouquet of flowers in my hand. What was I thinking? I glanced around. Maybe I could shove them under my seat when no one was looking.

That's when I noticed Sally Gertz sitting in the seat in front of me. Like everyone else, she was dressed up for her big-screen debut.

I leaned forward and tapped her shoulder. "Mrs. Gertz?"

She looked back. "Yes?"

"Remember that realistic fall you did at the beginning of the movie?" I didn't wait for her reply. Instead I handed her the flowers. "These are for a fine actress at her movie premiere."

Mrs. Gertz gasped. "Why, thank you, Frank."

I patted her shoulder and leaned back in my chair. As I glanced over, I saw Joe smiling at me.

"Nice," he whispered.

I smiled back and then settled in to watch the movie.